IF IT WASN'T FOR THE MONEY

A Sam Anderson Mystery

by J. A. Martine

Published by:
Wood Dragon Books
Post Office Box 1216
Regina, Saskatchewan, Canada S4P3B4
All rights reserved.

Copyright © 2014 by Jeanne Martinson
ISBN: 978-0-9685370-7-7

Without limiting the rights under copyright reserved above, no part of this publication may be reproduced, stored in or introduced into a retrieval system or transmitted in any form, or by any means (electronic, mechanical, photocopying, recording, or otherwise) without the prior written permission of both the copyright owner and the above publisher of this book.

This is a work of fiction. Names, characters and incidents are either the product of the author's imagination or used fictitiously. Any exceptions to this rule are noted in the back section "Author's Note - Real or Not".

For more information on the author, see j-a-martine.com.

ACKNOWLEDGEMENTS

First, thank you to my early readers – Pat Dell, Jennifer Pierce, Nancy Bowey, Gale Wilkie and Carole Stepenoff. Special thanks to Carole who brought the manuscript to her book club – their feedback was vital in the rewriting for the third draft.

Thank you to Jill Dand and Teresa Shepit who were responsible for the cover and interior design. Thank you to Shanaya Nelson for her work on the e-book production.

Thank you to friends and family who sparked ideas for plot or character development, especially Dustin Chubb, Carla McEachern, Dave Rodwell and Alda Bouvier.

Thanks to PD James who gave me an insightful few minutes of her time. Without her encouragement, this book would not have begun.

Lastly, thank you to my husband, Malcolm Bucholtz. What a source of information, editing and encouragement you have been! No writer could have asked for a better collaborator.

PROLOGUE

Day Five

Aboard the ship Sea Wanderer

2 a.m.

The man in the dark suit grabbed the lapels of the white uniform jacket worn by the Captain of the Sea Wanderer and shook the garment. His eyes bored into the Captain's.

"My wife is on the ship. My wife is not on the ship. Which is it Captain? Where exactly is my wife?"

The Captain stepped back, pulling his uniform jacket free from the other's grip. He smoothed his lapels with his palms and took a notebook from his inside pocket.

"According to our security personnel, she disembarked

yesterday morning at 1000 hours and re-boarded yesterday at 1500 hours. You made us aware of her disappearance at 2200 last evening." The captain returned the notebook to his inside pocket.

Taking a deep breath, he looked the other man directly in the eyes, and said quietly, "Since that time, we have searched extensively for her in every area of the ship. She simply seems to have vanished."

Day One

Aboard the ship Sea Wanderer
and
leaving Vancouver

*Slow Roasted Rack of Pork with
Wild Mushroom Ragout,
Scallion Potatoes and Guinness Sauce*

Or

*Whole Roasted Sirloin of Beef with
Yorkshire Pudding,
Caramelized Root Vegetables*

Or

*Grilled Fresh Pacific Salmon with
Lobster Mousse,
Tarragon New Potatoes*

CHAPTER ONE

She woke suddenly, her cry disappearing into a ragged inhale. She swung her legs over the side of the bed and pulled the white terry cloth robe closer. For a moment, she was still in the dream and the unfamiliar room confused her.

The dream was always the same. Tristan wrapped in a dirty blanket on the floor of a stolen van, his breath gone, his short life prematurely ended. She awoke at the same moment each time in the dream, at the point where the police officer pulled back the blanket and she saw her baby nephew's face.

She walked to the minute stateroom washroom and stepped into the even smaller shower. An hour later, the emotional remnants of the dream were gone and she was ready to face an evening with strangers. She reminded herself she likes strangers. Strangers like her company. Her life was all about making friends with strangers.

CHAPTER TWO

Sam Anderson lifted the pashmina off the bed and draped it over her shoulders. The soft green wool matched her eyes and the green and white design of her sheath dress. After one last look in the mirror to ensure she was presentable, she combed a few runaway auburn strands back into their sleek bob and smoothed her lipstick by rubbing her lips together. With a smile to herself, she turned from the mirror and escaped the small stateroom.

She walked towards the aft of the ship, ignoring the guide rails to her left and right. She automatically shifted to her sea legs, moving with the rhythmic roll of the Sea Wanderer as the waves, ever so slightly, tilted the ship from starboard to port and port to starboard. She watched the first time passengers hold fast to the guide rails along the cabin passageway. Only three hours from port, she thought, and the sea was already separating out the strong from the poorly balanced.

Turning from the passageway flanked by cabin doors, Sam took a quick flight of stairs down to emerge into the grand lobby with its elegant multi-level staircase and access to the public areas of the ship. This and the higher two decks held pubs and bars, a casino, a theatre, several chef-named restaurants, and exclusive shops; not to mention multiple temporary photography studios offering the ever present opportunity to be photographed with your fellow travelers by a ship's professional paparazzo.

The air buzzed with the excitement of the first time passengers, eager to discover every nook and cranny of the floating hotel. *No doubt several will be genuinely surprised and pleased when they return to their staterooms after the evening's cabaret show,* she thought with a smile, *to find an animal figure created out of their cabin's bath towel sitting patiently on their turned down bedcovers.*

She wandered over to the evening's menu posted beside the large double doors to the main restaurant. The casual dining option of 24-hour buffet grazing appealed to younger families and large groups. But some travellers were drawn to the formality and calm of the main full service dining restaurant and that included Sam. "Appetizers – Southwest Roasted Peppers and Avocado Salad, Moroccan Spiced Ahi Tuna Loin with Olive Tapenade," she read. *Oh no, bring on the shapewear.*

The main restaurant on the Sea Wanderer held tables set in twos, fours, sixes, and eights. Unless you were a consumer of many voyages, you were destined for a table of six or eight. The few tables of two were reserved for long-term clients or those well known to the cruise line. Although Sam may have qualified for a quieter dinner experience, she looked forward to what her table of six may offer. She had taken many cruises as a travel writer and was always amazed at the variety of people she met and the quirks and opinions they revealed over the several nights of food selection, alcohol consumption and forced conversation.

The culinary choices and amusing dinner companions were fixtures of all cruises. What drew Sam to this particular ship and this cruise was the desire to experience and write about the sport of rock rappelling. Writing as a travel journalist for Out of the Ordinary Travel Adventures, or OOTA magazine, had led her to many out of the ordinary spots. On the surface, a cruise ship wouldn't be noted for being particularly 'out of the ordinary,' but she was determined that her article on the unique activities available on the Alaskan cruise's ashore excursions would be.

Her editor at OOTA had arranged for her complimentary week aboard in a ship-promotion contract. Although she was required to present two workshops on travel photography as part of her contract, the rest of her time was her own and her focus would be writing and photographing the ashore activities that would appeal to the more active and curious traveller. So, rappelling down the side of an Alaskan mountain was on the agenda.

CHAPTER THREE

Rupert Williams finished unpacking his toiletries in the miniscule stateroom washroom, smacking his elbows on two separate walls. Rubbing each elbow, he cursed the space. If at 5 feet 10 inches he felt confined, he could only imagine how irritated his much taller brother-in-law, Daniel, next door would be with the compact accommodations. He chuckled to himself. His brother-in-law was a rather smug, annoying snot and Rupert felt a small jolt of amusement over any discomfort Daniel may experience.

For a moment Rupert's amusement over Daniel's vexation distracted him from the ever-present weariness brought on by his current financial situation. Reality settled over him like a dull cloud and his smile dissolved into a grimace.

In the beginning of their relationship his wife, Lauren, and he faced the world together from a shared financial footing. But the financial circumstances created by the death of her parents several years ago triggered a nag at his self-confidence that eventually spiralled down into the financial crisis in which he presently found himself.

With her parents' death, Lauren and her sister, Kathleen, inherited not only millions of dollars but became co-CEOs of an organization that was funded by the annual investment returns on those millions. In theory, his wife had access to millions of dollars. However, both she and her sister only saw themselves as stewards of the funds, not as recipients.

He found the situation both frustrating and emasculating. He couldn't access the funds to live the kind of life he thought they both deserved. Nor could he earn enough money in his position as a business loans officer to create a lifestyle that competed with the shadow of those millions. He would rather that the millions didn't exist.

A year ago, he was talked into a high stakes poker game with his new brother-in-law, Daniel. Daniel staked him for the fun of it, he said. He wanted at least one friendly face around the table. Rupert had won the pot. The next week, Daniel invited him again but said he wasn't staking his competition, so if Rupert wanted in the game he needed to bring his own funds. Rupert had already spent most of the money from the previous week's win on an expensive dinner out with Lauren, but he had enough for the $500 stake.

For several weeks, Rupert won at the weekly game. Eventually the players around the table asked him to go find his fun elsewhere. He decided to try the casino a few streets over from his downtown Vancouver office. The Edgewater Casino overlooking False Creek had a high stakes poker room and he was quickly drawn into a weekly game with a group of players.

He was a consistent winner and was beginning to enjoy the extras he could spend on himself and Lauren.

Although he consciously knew that he was trying to balance the financial scales between Lauren and himself through this gambling effort, he was still amazed at his own impulsiveness. His history was one of even mindedness and caution when it came to money.

His mother had been a stage actress and he was raised around creative people who desired financial success, but not at the loss of creative freedom or critical acclaim. As a teenager living in London's west end, he took care of his family's finances, stretching a dollar from his mother's feast or famine income, negotiating the rent with the landlord, and saying no to his mother's spending sprees and emotional purchases. Rupert had inherited his financial skills from his long gone father, she claimed, as she certainly didn't possess them. From his mother, he inherited an appreciation for their home country of England, a positive attitude in the face of disaster, and an ability to make others laugh.

His gambling luck had turned when a group from his weekly game started meeting in a hotel room at the Pan Pacific Hotel six weeks ago. Each week he fell deeper and deeper into debt. He had maxed out his line of credit at the bank where he worked and had taken cash advances on his credit cards. The debt servicing would soon be beyond what he could cover with his paycheque.

As a bonded employee at the bank, he needed a clean credit rating and a Beacon credit score of 700. Once he started making late payments or missing payments, his job would be in jeopardy. On top of his gambling debt and credit problems, he was feeling the added pressure of possible unemployment.

The week before he had sat in a meeting where the CEO had spoken about the upcoming merger with two smaller financial institutions. Rupert had a degree in Finance, but lacked the seniority of most of the other business loans officers. When he asked his senior manager about his job security, he was told that no one's role was safe and if he saw something available elsewhere he should jump at it.

Rupert wondered sometimes if the hotel where he had his weekly game was bad luck itself, or if the players were not above board. Yet, he could not see any cheating if it was occurring.

His natural optimistic nature fought against the oppressive weight, creating a small space of blue sky in his mind. He needed to get out of this credit card debt hole, re-inflate his line of credit and find a new employment position.

Luckily, he had such a possibility. For over a year, Daniel had been nudging him to help convince their wives to permit Daniel's brokerage firm to handle the investments of the 'bloody millions.' Daniel had assured Rupert that there would be a significant position with his firm if Rupert could assist him in this endeavour. And at a significant salary compared to the bank where he currently toiled. Rupert had mentioned Daniel's idea to his wife several times, but she insisted that Kathleen would never go for the idea so there was no point pursuing it. It made sense to her, she agreed, but those decisions were Kathleen's, not hers.

Yes, his life had gone all pear-shaped. But, he reminded himself, there was action that could be taken.

A week on a ship with a casino, he thought, rubbing his hands together in anticipation before picking up his tie. *A wonderful chance to change my luck. Surely a week will be time enough to get out of the deepest part of this hole. I have just had a bad run that's all. A bloody bad run. I just need to stay positive. Everyone has a bad run now and then. Mine has just run longer than ever before. I should never have gotten involved with that game at the hotel. I should have stuck with the chaps in the poker room at the casino. And a week to convince Kathleen and Lauren to give Daniel a chance at making those 'bloody millions' grow. What is wrong with that?*

Rupert felt very positive about this week at sea. He was going to succeed. He just felt it.

He drew his tie through its final loop and tightened it around his shirt collar, wiggling his chin as he settled the knot.

His thoughts turned to dinner and the evening ahead. *Who would be at their dinner table besides the four of them this evening? Maybe someone who might like a friendly hand of poker, or bet on a game of gin?* Rupert was a flexible gambler if there ever was one. Pulling his jacket from the confined stateroom closet, he tapped the inside pocket to ensure a deck of cards was present. He slipped on the jacket and smiled at his wife.

As usual, she wore her blonde hair down, in natural soft curls around her face. When they first met, her curls had been short little corkscrews that made her look fun and approachable. He remembered the literature class he couldn't escape in university. He had been ruing the first year liberal art class requirement, when those little curls sat beside him and his heart was lost forever to any other.

Today's longer curls were more sophisticated, trailing beyond her chin and shoulders, the corkscrews pulled down into soft coils due to the weight. Regardless of the length, those curls tempted him. He knew how they felt against his fingers. Like silk, smooth, soft, flexible. *What was she doing with him?* he wondered. *How would he hold on to her if he was fired?*

CHAPTER FOUR

Lauren stood on the balcony of the stateroom, finishing her glass of red wine and thinking. She only needed to put her passport and wallet in the stateroom safe before she and Rupert joined her sister, Kathleen, and Kathleen's husband, Daniel for dinner. Her sister was on her mind and she was perplexed as to what direction to take to help her.

She looked at her passport picture and then closed the identification document with a slap. *Identity is a strange thing*, thinking about her twin sister down the passageway. *Who am I separate from her?* she thought. *Who is she separate from me?*

To others, they seemed very similar. They both had naturally curly blonde hair, even though their stylists cut and highlighted their locks slightly differently. They shared soft blue-grey eyes, high cheekbones and slightly pointed and determined chins.

To each other, they seemed both identical and foreign. Similar in looks, dissimilar in talents and temperament. Lauren was artistic and was often characterized by others as emotional. Kathleen was seen as logical and, usually, the more sensible of the two.

Each sister's happiness meant as much to the other as her own. When one was upset, the other mirrored the emotion. Lauren had been feeling Kathleen's anxiety and withdrawal for months now and the negative feelings were increasing. Although Kathleen had said nothing to her about the cause of her distress, Lauren was certain Daniel was the source of her sister's sorrow.

Lauren sighed. She couldn't live her sister's life for her, or make decisions about Kathleen and Daniel's marriage. She could only be supportive.

I am going to make sure this cruise turns out to be everything Kathleen wishes. Lauren rolled her shoulders, sloughing off her own trepidation. *After all, it is my responsibility. I was born 10 minutes sooner.*

Inside the cabin, she tossed her passport and wallet into the waiting safe and set the code. She smiled at Rupert as he shrugged on his suit jacket. She sighed, rubbed his arms and moved in for an embrace. Her height in heels matched her to her husband's height exactly. She thought that was quite perfect. She didn't have to lift her lips to be covered by Rupert's quick but warm caress. Her marriage seemed so secure and loving compared to her sister's. She sighed again in contentment before pulling away.

"Well honey, ready for an adventure?" he asked.

"I sure am," she replied.

He plucked her miniature purse off the bed, tucked in her plastic stateroom key, and struck a theatrical pose with the fashion item under his arm. She laughed at his tomfoolery, took the beaded item and preceded him out of the stateroom.

Rupert's upbringing surrounded by theatrical personalities occasionally erupted, overcoming his left-brain love of mathematics and all things logical and reasonable. His sporadic outrageous behaviour was one of the many reasons she loved him.

"You always can make me laugh!" she cried, forgetting her sister's problems for brief moment.

CHAPTER FIVE

"A cruise, a damn cruise!" Daniel Zackery railed to nothing but the ocean. "A week away from the office with only exorbitantly priced internet and crappy mobile telephone service to compensate. This better be worth it." He sipped his martini and leaned out over the stateroom's balcony rail as the ship sailed under the Lion's Gate Bridge and pulled out to sea, leaving Vancouver behind.

His plan to woo his wife into agreement did not include watching lumberjack shows, panning for gold or eating smoked salmon around a fire. He wasn't interested in what he considered campy, touristy events and he knew his impatience would reflect badly upon his character. Claiming work commitments, he had convinced the rest of their group of four to go on the ashore excursions without him when they docked in Skagway, Juneau and Ketchikan.

His work claim was true. His career and entire financial

worth would be going south if he didn't find a solution soon. He needed to get Kathleen to sign the papers on this trip. Time was running out.

His boutique investment firm was close to bankruptcy, thanks to his optimistic, yet tragic, deal making prior to the 2008 crash. He had invested heavily in two private start-up companies, assuming that once they went public he would make considerable return. Unfortunately, one had fizzled and one had exploded.

On top of those challenges, he was extended with a personal deal with 'the boys.'

The scene from the Cambridge Resource Show the week before was engraved in his mind. Investor relations people from financially distressed junior mineral companies dodged direct questions from worried seasoned investors, but continued to spin tales of imminent major new wealth-creating discoveries just around the corner to naïve new investors. He understood their desperation because he was feeling plenty of his own.

He had come to the show to meet with his investment colleagues. A consortium of like-minded, well-funded gentlemen who played the rise and fall of the fragile resource market. They not only played the waves of the rise and fall of the resource market, they created the waves, making massive financial gains as a stock soared and then exiting quickly with massive profits, which generally created a free-fall of the stock price. This pump and dump of a stock could only happen with aggressively-marketed, small-cap stocks in a market where finding the next gold discovery and getting in on the bottom floor stoked the testosterone and raised the blood pressure of the investing male. It was just sexy.

Daniel was desperate. He committed to the boys last pump

and dump scheme – a gold exploration company working a project in Ghana. They had covered his purchase of 1,000,000 shares at 7 cents but now they were asking for reimbursement. His time was running out. He had maximized his lines of credit and fully mortgaged his Vancouver condo. He just didn't have enough money to cover the commitment.

Once he paid the boys, and they pushed the stock price up, he would sell out. The profits from this pump and dump would keep his ship above water and what he had lined up on the horizon would make it buoyant.

Many junior mining companies were looking desperately for new drilling and mineral properties, such as the deal in Ghana. But a few publicly traded mining corporations were recognizing that the mining business was not going to turn around quickly. Intelligent men like himself, he admitted, were looking towards a different future. He planned to match the regulated, public corporate structure of a few beaten down junior mining companies with the emerging legal drug business of marijuana. The demand for the product was a given, only to grow larger as more American states and Canadian provinces jumped on the bandwagon towards decriminalization and deregulation of the wonderful miracle weed. The marijuana growers were looking for a legal, fast way to go public and the mining companies were looking for a way to stay in business. It would be a perfect win. A win for the pot growers, a win for the dispensary operators in Colorado and Washington, a win for the beaten-up junior mining stock and especially a nice win for him.

He smiled. He would make more money than his father or any of his brothers. He would be the family financial success story.

But time was running out. Although his purpose in marrying

Kathleen a year ago was to ensure that he eventually had full control over the investing of the millions she managed, he needed to accelerate the plan.

The high-risk investors at Zackery Investments who had given him a comfortable living in commissions as they traded in and out of his mining stock recommendations were nervous. The junior mining sector was struggling. Clients were shoring up their investment portfolios by moving their assets into the safety of money market funds. This was putting a serious dent in the commission stream Daniel needed to pay for the lifestyle he enjoyed. As his income decreased, he had dipped into his personal funds to maintain his business and personal lifestyle. He had dipped to the point that the well had run dry.

At the resource show, he had found the gentlemen he sought and had confirmed he would have the money by the deadline. He only managed to play with the big boys and be invited into their private, lucrative and sketchy opportunities because of their perception of his overblown assets.

They believed that he already controlled the assets Kathleen managed and co-owned with her sister. That was the only reason he had been invited to participate and the only reason he was being given an extension.

But his time was running out. He only had 19 days. Kathleen had to be convinced.

This trip for the two couples was a time and financial sacrifice on his part. The goal was to appear to the other three parties as a loving, caring spouse. Kathleen had been distancing herself from him, emotionally and physically. He needed her by his side, financially and legally, at least until he was clear from his current financial debris. A cruise to Alaska seemed a waste of good time and money, but was a drop in the bucket compared to the funds he needed to fulfill his commitment to the investment deal and keep his firm afloat.

His preference for a holiday location certainly would have been different, but he knew neither Rupert nor the twins could get away for more than a week at last minute, and leaving from and returning to Vancouver was certainly convenient for all concerned.

Last month he had put the wheels in motion to put Rupert in financial straits and he knew that his brother-in-law's bank was also under massive change. Last week, he told Rupert that if the twins decided to hire Daniel's firm to manage the millions, Daniel would find a well-placed and well-paid position for Rupert in Zackery Investments. Daniel hoped that Rupert had already begun talking to Lauren about moving the funds to his firm. Although Kathleen controlled the financial arrangements, she needed Lauren's approval for any significant change. Lauren's advocating for the funds to be moved to Daniel's care would also weigh with Kathleen.

No, Daniel thought, *I will pass on the family outings ashore and focus on spending time with my wife dancing in the evening and taking starlit walks. Places where we can be intimately connected. Where I can hold her in my arms and remind her why she fell in love with me.*

Kathleen. Even once this crisis was over and her money had re-established his firm, he didn't want to let her go. The doors that had opened to him just by being her husband were startling. There was a tight knit philanthropic group in the Vancouver community who supported each other's charitable efforts. They invited each other to fundraising events where they networked and developed business relationships. Life was greatly improved, financially and socially, by being the husband of Kathleen Corey Zackery. They were becoming one of the A-list couples with increasing social 'Q.' Kathleen was even dressing and presenting herself less as the CEO of a child-focused charity and more as the wife of a powerful financial player.

I just need to manage Kathleen better, he resolved. During their last conversation about the management of the funds, she had suggested that they should have some time apart. He had lost control during that conversation and hurt her, which wasn't what he had intended. He wanted her to respect and trust him. Perhaps sometimes he became over-demanding, but he couldn't risk driving her away. Since their last disagreement, he had activated the GPS tracking indicator on her IPhone as well as the GPS tracker on her car. He wanted to know where she was, 24 hours a day. If she decided to leave him, it wouldn't be long before he would know where to find her.

He needed control over that financial portfolio. He had plans not only to solve his current situation but he had future plans for the funds that supported the foundation. If he could control and invest the millions the way he would like, he could be involved in any deal.

I just need to appear to be a better husband, he reminded himself. *Certainly I can pull off a week being the perfect spouse.* He threw back the remainder of the martini and went inside to maximize his plan.

CHAPTER SIX

Kathleen swirled her long blonde hair into a smooth French roll and inserted hairpins to secure the strands. She sprayed it thoroughly to ensure no errant hairs would escape. Her preference would be to wear it down and loose, but Daniel liked it up, saying it looked more professional and elegant.

For the past year, she had dressed and groomed herself more and more to Daniel's liking and less to her own. In most situations, her opinion was not very different than his. When their opinions clashed, going along was easiest. When she felt very different in the judgement of a situation and spoke up, she was often ridiculed or sarcastically corrected. She was speaking up less and less and going along more and more.

This was not how she thought marriage would be. This was not the marriage she saw her parents enjoy. She was not the woman she had been. She wondered where she had gone wrong. God wasn't giving her any answers.

Although she had given into Daniel on almost all subjects, she had denied him one of the requests he desired most. To help manage the millions that she and her sister Lauren inherited from her parents and which funded the non-profit organization, The Corey Art Project. As in their parents' time, Lauren and Kathleen invested the money in an ethical, conservative way. All interest and revenue was donated to the Corey Art Project while the principal remained intact from year to year.

Both daughters, like their parents before them, were paid a more than reasonable salary from the Corey Art Project organization and worked full-time in its efforts.

From the beginning of their relationship, Daniel had disagreed with her investing the funds in conservative low risk investments. As time went on, he became more insistent that he help her in searching out more profitable ventures to invest in. She was a chartered accountant and he had an MBA. Together, he claimed, they would create the perfect team to ensure increased funding for the Corey Art Project. He appealed to her logic and business sense. However, Kathleen felt that not to follow her parents' and aunt's vision for the Corey Art Project and their strategy for investment of the millions were wrong. Daniel's disapproval was the price for her consistency to her parents' and aunt's vision.

The millions. The damn millions, as her brother-in-law Rupert called them. They were a blessing for the good they did but could be a curse for the chaos they created personally.

She stepped into a long sleeved little black dress. She swirled her hips and the flared skirt settled into place. Although it was a warm evening leaving Vancouver, the long sleeves were necessary. Daniel's fingerprint marks were still visible from their conversation when she had brought up the idea of a possible separation.

He wouldn't give her one, he had said, not now and not ever. He loved her, he had said, and would try harder to make her happy. He would make her happy, he had insisted. She just sometimes angered him. He had offered the cruise for them and her sister and brother-in-law. To take her mind off their disagreement, he had said. So that she knew he was sorry that it had all gotten out of hand, he had said. She had managed to appear grateful when he proposed the idea at the time, but she worried the simmering and tightly held anger he felt over her resistance would not decrease.

She was beginning to feel that she was no longer safe. He was so unlike the man she had married barely a year ago. Where was the agreeable, supportive man she fell in love with? He had been such a good friend following her parents' death. He had even volunteered to be on the Corey Art Project committee for fundraising. It had seemed a natural action to take when he asked her out and a year later to wed. Not only was he supportive of her dreams and the work she did, he was a loving partner and caring lover.

She looked in the mirror and shook her finger at her reflection. Did God want her to stay in this marriage? Perhaps he could send a sign. She shook her head to clear her thoughts. Regardless of the future, tonight she was on a cruise with her sister. She smiled into the mirror.

Daniel entered the cabin from the veranda deck and she turned at the sound. Her smile faltered and she straightened her shoulders.

She was not going to be one of those women. A woman who has a husband who tracks her moves, even though she knew that Daniel had begun to. A woman who takes the blame for things that goes wrong, even though she knows she was not at fault. She wasn't going to be one of those women who just go along with what her husband wants, even though for the past six months she had done just that in most circumstances. She wasn't going to be one of those women who put up with being bruised, justifying that her husband was just very upset at the moment. She wasn't going to wear long sleeves to hide marks, even though she knew she was doing just that. She wasn't going to be one of those women who hid her life from her family because she was ashamed or scared, even though she knew she had been pushing Lauren away.

She wasn't going to be one of those women. Anymore.

CHAPTER SEVEN

Although the sitting was for 8 p.m., Sam was eager to find out the gastronomic selections of the evening and was one of the first in line to be seated at her pre-assigned table. She followed her white-coated server through the maze of dining room tables to the far wall, which wasn't a wall at all but a bank of large windows showing the fierce froth generated by the propellers and hull. She watched the parallel lines discharged from the back of the ship and the massive bubbles of the wake.

Far from the main doors and at back of the ship, her designated table provided an interesting view of the action in the room. Sam settled into her chair with her back to the sea. The two-storied Olympus Restaurant held up to 800 guests per sitting. The servers, sommeliers, and busboys were streams of white ribbons in their formal uniforms as they sat passengers at their designated tables and then returned to the maître d' for more hungry guests.

Perusing the menu, she was deciding between the Whole

Roasted Sirloin of Beef with Yorkshire Pudding and the Grilled Fresh Pacific Salmon with Lobster Mousse as an entrée when her server returned, followed closely by several of her dining companions.

The group of two men and two women descended on the table. The first man had a bored look on his face and a firm grip on his companion's elbow, choosing a chair for her and then holding it for her to sit. The server held the chair for the second woman and then offered menus to the new guests. The two men sat, one to the left and one to the right of Sam.

The men could not have been more different and the women more alike. The man so conscientious of assisting his companion was in a well-cut dark suit with a collarless silk shirt of the same black. He had a good four inches in height over the second man and held himself with a careless elegance and perhaps even arrogance. He was blond, tanned and possessed what her mother would have called Paul Newman eyes.

Pulling herself away from those stormy baby blues, she watched the other man settle in his seat, pulling the cloth napkin into his lap. He was dressed very conventionally in a white shirt, blue and red striped tie and navy suit. He had chocolate brown hair and eyes to match. His hair was cut short except for the front lock, which he immediately pushed back into place after it flopped forward when he sat down. He reached out to Sam and offered his hand.

Introducing himself as Rupert and his wife as Lauren-Jennifer, he was quickly interrupted by his blonde wife who with a shake of her head set her long hair and bouncy bangs swinging. "Kathleen and I both were given hyphenated names, but everyone just calls me Lauren and Kathleen-Barbra Kathleen," she tagged on,

"Double hyphenated Lauren-Jennifer Corey-Williams is much too much of a mouthful."

The second woman extended her hand and introduced her husband, Daniel Zackery and herself, Kathleen. Her hair was the same colour as the other woman's, but in a French roll that elongated her neck and gave her a regal, quiet air. Her face held the same features in the same way as the other woman. They were most likely sisters, even possibly twins.

"Barbra or Barbara?" Sam asked.

"Oh no! Barbra like Streisand not like Stanwyck!" replied Lauren for Kathleen. "Mother had seen Streisand in the movie *The Way We Were* a few years before we were born and so named one of us Barbra after Barbra Streisand. Whenever she was asked whether Barbra was two or three syllables, she would simply reply 'Like Streisand, not Stanwyck.'"

"However," interrupted Kathleen with a smile, "fewer and fewer people remember who Barbara Stanwyck was, so the line is becoming dated. One day we will have to explain the line that is to there to explain the name." The twins looked at each other and laughed at the inside family story.

"And your second name, Lauren? After anyone famous?" Sam asked.

"Only to our family. A long dead aunt."

Rupert added, "A rich long dead aunt."

"Actually," Lauren continued, elbowing her husband in the forearm. "She began the arts organization for at risk youth that our parents ran until they passed on and that Kathleen and I now run."

"How interesting! How does it work?" Sam asked with anticipation.

"Excuse me." For the first time, Daniel spoke. With a nod to the waiter, "Can we hold off getting to know our new friend until we order beverages?"

Sam wondered if he was thirsty or just tired of the women's conversation. She felt somehow responsible for the slight tension that now hung over the table. After the drink orders had been made, she apologetically inserted, "Partly my fault – I'm always asking questions. I'm a travel writer so I am very interested in people and what they like and are curious about."

"Well," jumped in Rupert, "what I am curious about is whether we are to have a sixth at the table or if we are a man out, as it were. Not that Daniel and I aren't able to hold up our end of the conversation." His accented words played across the table and Sam reminded herself to ask him later what part of the United Kingdom he was originally from.

Right on the heels of his comment, a short fellow who had a casual mussed air about himself plunked down in the empty chair between the two blondes. Giving a smile around the table, he swung his suit jacket off and placed it on the chair back. He picked up his napkin and dabbed his flushed cheeks and forehead.

"Sorry for the late arrival, got delayed in the shops. Do you know there is a $10 shop here with jewellery and what have you? I have already done my Christmas shopping, six months ahead of time and we have barely left port!"

Daniel looked at the new arrival and lifted one eyebrow. *I have a feeling I will be seeing a lot of that raised eyebrow this week,* thought Sam. *I just hope I won't be the source of his attention and the recipient of that particular muscular facial move.*

Day Two

Aboard the ship Sea Wanderer
and
Sailing The Inside Passage

*Pan Roasted Duck Breast with
Dried Apricot Croquettes,
Brandy and Blackberry Jus*

Or

*Grilled Sea Bass
with Young Vegetables and Béarnaise Sauce*

Or

*Spinach Ravioli with Cherry Tomatoes
and Balsamic and Parmesan Cream*

CHAPTER EIGHT

"Oh that was so interesting!" Lauren had attended the first of Sam's photography workshops and cornered her at the end of the hour. "I have so many questions! Can we get a coffee and talk more?"

"Certainly. What were you wondering about?"

After two cups of coffee and an hour of Q & A later, Lauren put down her cup with a sigh. "I can see by cropping the photo tighter and moving the subject focus into a corner, I can paint the actual frame to extend the subject and create another dimension. I am used to working in one medium at a time – a photo, watercolour or oil."

Sam nodded. "By having the wooden frame itself as part of the art canvass, you can go beyond photo, watercolour and even oil to other mediums that extend the picture. You could use fabric or earth materials like shells, twigs, even..."

"Bottle caps?" Lauren laughed.

"Whatever the artist wants."

"This would be a very interesting process for the kids at the Corey Art Project. The photos are what they see in their life now and the watercolour or oil on the frame could represent what their future may be. That idea has real therapy possibilities. Thank you so much. I know I've probably taken up more of your time than you bargained on."

"Well that is the beauty of a full day at sea. No way to go ashore even if you wished to do so. Except for the class I just taught I have no obligations today."

"I was just thinking it would be a good day to find a quiet place to read a book."

Sam grinned. "I tried that earlier today, and guess who found me? Our dinner companion George! That fellow is one enthusiastic traveller.

"You think he was excited about the discount jewellery store? He's going to attend the first showings of each movie in the cinema to, and I quote, 'get my money's worth!'" Sam concluded, making quote marks in the air.

"He is quite funny," Lauren agreed. "I enjoyed his company at dinner. I think we all did, except maybe Daniel. But then Daniel is used to more seriously minded company."

"What exactly does Daniel do?" Sam asked Lauren.

"He runs a boutique investment firm in Vancouver."

"Ooh, that does sound serious."

"His family back east has always been in banking or investing. After he went to Upper Canada College he took his degree in Business at University of Toronto and then his MBA at Simon Fraser in Vancouver and just stayed out here. He obviously is very good at what he does, as his company seems quite successful.

"He is always sponsoring charity events, often at the highest sponsorship levels. As humourless as he often seems, those yin acts of kindness go a little way in balancing out the yang aggression of how he does everything else."

Sam thought about Yin and Yang, the Asian concept of two complementary forces that make up all aspects of life. "Maybe making money just makes him serious!" she laughed.

Lauren nodded with a smile. "This is the first time that he has invited Rupert and me along on a holiday where he paid the tab. He said he wanted to take us all on a family vacation. I don't expect to see much of Daniel except at the dinner table in the evening though. He may be away from the work but the work isn't away from him."

"It was nice of him to bring you, though," Sam said.

"It was, wasn't it? I can't believe I am telling you all this. You certainly are a good listener. You must be a great interviewer."

Sam smiled. Lauren was like many people. One question lit a match for an explosive diatribe or unblocked a waterfall of closely held information. The sympathetic, trustworthy listener was all that was required.

"I hope you didn't feel interrogated. I am curious about the world around me and the people in it. That is the best part of being a writer, running into the most interesting people who all have a story to tell and a life that they have lived."

"No, it is just me really, I run off at the mouth. Kathleen is the introverted accountant and I am the extroverted artist. Ever since we were small, I spoke for the both of us. And she thinks for the both of us," she laughed.

"What are your plans for tomorrow when we dock in Skagway?" Sam asked.

"Kathleen and I are going ashore and Daniel and Rupert are staying on the ship. Rupert said there was some activity he was interested in and Daniel is only interested in his computer so I expect he will be hanging out somewhere close to internet service. I don't know why he even came along if he is going to only spend time with us in the evening," she added slightly resentfully.

"How long have Kathleen and Daniel been married?" Sam asked, curious about the lives of her dinner mates.

"They met three years ago at a fundraiser for our organization and were married a year ago this spring. He seemed very interested in building relationships with charities and being seen as a philanthropic contributor in Vancouver.

"I think she first dated him because he was so interested in our charity and seemed to enjoy the kinds of things she was interested in. I think their first date was the play 'As You Like It' at the Bard on the Beach Shakespeare Festival. Their second date was at the VSO – the Vancouver Symphony Orchestra. But I don't think live theatre and Mozart are true interests of his."

"So he tricked her into dinner dates under false pretences?"

"Tricked her all the way to the altar and then let his true colours show."

"I guess some men are willing to go to those extremes. I certainly know of women who didn't let their husbands see them without makeup until the day after the wedding," added Sam. She chuckled but Lauren frowned and shook her head.

Eager to put the conversation into a lighter mood, Sam asked, "Can you tell me about this charity, the Corey Art Project. What does it do and who does it help?"

"My aunt Jennifer started the foundation and when she passed on, Mom and Dad ran it until their deaths a few years ago. The mandate is to provide visual art opportunities for kids who have neither financial resources nor family support to engage in this type of art experience. We provide workshops for kids in at-risk communities across the country, train instructors and fundraise to pay for it all.

"Ouch – that sounded like the mission statement off our website. I think it was actually," she said laughing. "I am so used to putting on the official story." Lauren shook her head. "Anyway, that is really what we do. We help kids in need to get their lives back on track or to cope with unmanageable situations."

"Were you both working for the Art Project when your parents died?"

"Kathleen and I had just turned 30 but we felt we had enough education and experience to run the organization. Luckily we have been surrounded by good advisors and a dedicated staff. I have a strong visual arts background, particularly in watercolour. I teach classes, orient other instructors, and act as the staff members' sounding board when they run into a bit of a pickle."

"Pickle?"

"Well when you work with kids at risk, the day can bring anything and once children start using art to explain their world, sometimes an instructor feels they must intercede in the child's revelation of their reality. It could be a situation of abuse, or a kid's awareness of illegal issues their parents are involved in, or as in a case last week, a student was falling apart because his only family member, a grandmother, was dying of cancer and he didn't know how to help her or what would become of him."

Sam blinked. Lauren had changed before her eyes from the effervescent and carefree artist to a serious minded social worker.

"What part does Kathleen play?" Sam asked.

"She is the financial whiz. She manages the budgets, staff costs, real estate issues, investments and donation requests. It can be something over the top some days. Our emerging focus is to bring in more donations. With rising costs in every one of our cost centres, and decreasing interest rates on our core investment, the donation side is always the challenging one. Even with the serious millions Aunt Jennifer won in the lotto to begin the Art Project, we still need more donations to serve the communities we wish to expand to."

Lauren didn't notice the bobbling of Sam's cup and saucer. "Wow," she whispered, "that is quite a load you two carry."

"I am glad I am on the instruction and creative side of the work and that Kathleen manages payroll, vendors and investments. I know that Daniel has wanted to assist her with the investing side and has a strong business background, but sometimes he doesn't realize that the money really isn't our money. It is in our trust and care. Kathleen and I make a good salary but we take this very seriously. It is more than a job to us."

Sam drummed her fingers on the chair arm. "Besides OOTA, sometimes I write freelance articles on non-travel subjects for other magazines. I think there might be a story here about the impact of art on youth development. I could work your foundation in as an example and that would give your organization some profile. Let me think on it and see if I can figure out an angle."

"That would be great – I can't wait to tell Kathleen!" Lauren was up and off to find her twin.

Sam drank the last of the tea in her cup, thinking about lotteries and obligations.

CHAPTER NINE

Dinner the second night on ship followed the pattern of the first night. Sam arrived first, with time to slowly look at each appetizer, mulling over which of the many delicious choices she could embrace. "Steamed Fresh Black Mussels with White Wine and Parsley Cream Sauce or Cream of Green Asparagus Soup?" she read. *Wouldn't you hope that all black mussels are fresh?*

She had just settled on the soup when the two couples arrived. The five had just received their drink orders when a rumpled George arrived with a piece of white tape around the bridge of the nose of his eyeglasses. He plunked down into his chair and drew his white napkin across his lap.

"Sorry for the delay. You are not going to believe what happened to me today! I was out on my deck reading and forgot that I had closed the damn glass door to my cabin. I walked right into it! Nearly broke my nose! So I took the soap from the bathroom and wrote my name on the pane to make damn sure

I never did that again. Well if the cabin steward didn't wash the window and I ran into it again! My book flew out of my hand and went over the rail. I was right at the good part where I was figuring out who the killer was too. Damn it!"

Sam looked at Daniel to check on the elevation of his eyebrow. Yes, it was flying high.

"Well I can certainly see how that might be upsetting. Were you hurt?" asked Lauren.

"Only my pride, only my pride," he said with a wink, taking his menu from the patient server waiting beside his chair.

After the first course was served, George's natural curiosity took over the conversation. "So what did everyone do today?"

Sam jumped in, "I taught a photography class today. I have a second one scheduled the last full day at sea as well, if anyone is interested." She looked around the table with a grin. "But no pressure!

"I also lucked out today and found a great assistant to help me tomorrow when we stop in Skagway." She had scouted out her assistant, James, during her photography class. The class had gone well, with several serious photographers, some who were just starting out, and the remainder comprised of grandparents eager to learn how to crop pictures of their grandkids for annual Christmas letters. Every writing assignment came with its foibles and giving two photography classes during days at sea were a small price. And, it had netted her James.

"To carry things?" asked Kathleen.

"No, I can manage what I need to carry. I plan on climbing a granite mountain rock face and then rappelling down. I can't photograph myself and experience it at the same time so I will set up the shot and then clue in my new assistant, James, as to what to do with the camera."

"So you will climb up a mountain like Spiderman and drop back down?" asked Kathleen.

"Exactly, but probably with less grace. And several times perhaps to get the money shot."

"I am fascinated by photography but I am not very good at it. That is Lauren's arena of talent," commented Kathleen. "Do you have a dark room at home?"

"No, I'm rather homeless at the moment."

At the stunned expression around the table, Sam laughed.

"When I began travelling around the world for my work, I attempted to ensure my house in Saskatoon was taken care of. I would hire someone to check on the house, collect the mail, shovel the snow off the walks in the winter and cut the grass in the summer. But I was only home a few days a month and when I wasn't home, I worried that everything would be taken care of properly.

"When my water pipes froze and burst, leaving a flood in the basement, I threw in the home ownership towel. I returned home to destroyed belongings, a massive clean-up bill and a long list of required renos. So, instead of replacing most of my lost items, I fixed the water pipes, did the necessary renovations and listed the house. I have storage space in New Mexico for whatever I want to store and I travel with everything I truly need."

"Don't you have family in Saskatchewan?" Lauren asked, still shocked at Sam's wandering lifestyle.

"Not really." All of that was true, Sam sighed to herself. She was homeless. The flood only made the decision to sell her house and turn her back on the city of Saskatoon easier. She had no one back in Saskatchewan that wanted to see her. She had no family to return to, or more precisely, no family who wished to see her return. Tristan's death had changed a close-knit clan into a group of combatants.

At her comment, George looked thoughtful, cocking his head to look at her more closely. "Why New Mexico?"

"Far enough away from snow and frozen pipes?" laughed Lauren.

"The magazine I write the most for, OOTA, has its head office in New Mexico. My editor has a key to my storage unit and religiously deposits any travel memorabilia or documents I send her," responded Sam.

Lauren sent Sam a sad look. "It seems so solitary. Will you ever settle down again and have a home?"

"I make friends everywhere I go. I am not alone. Nor am I lonely. It wouldn't make sense to have a place as long as I am on the road this much. In the future, perhaps."

"You can't be working 365 days a year," accused Daniel.

"Two thirds of the year or so. I also spend time with friends here and there and a month in the south of France every winter with some other journalists."

"South of France. Hmm. I am surprised that travel writing and photography would pay that well," Daniel responded.

Sam looked at the soaring eyebrow. "I also write freelance for several magazines."

Lauren jumped in, "Sam might write an article on art foundations such as the Corey Art Project and profile who we are and how we raise our money and the good we do. Wouldn't that be fantastic?"

"Shit!" said Daniel under his breath. *All I need is for the funding structure of the money and the Art Project to become more public than it already is! Running out of time.*

Sitting to his immediate left, Sam lifted her own sardonic eyebrow at the quiet curse. She wondered what that comment was all about.

Day Three

Ashore in Skagway
and
Aboard the ship Sea Wanderer

Pork Medallion Oscar topped with Crabmeat, Sage and Brandy Sauce

Or

Caramelized Leek & Goat Cheese Tart, Citrus and White Truffle Oil

Or

Steak Diane with Pont Neuf Potatoes and Cognac Mushroom Sauce

CHAPTER TEN

Rupert threw down his poker hand and walked away from the table. Damn, he thought for sure this was going to be his day. He felt so confident that the gambling gods were with him today that he had maximized the cash advance on his only remaining credit card with credit available.

He told Lauren that he had something he wanted to take in on the ship so she and Kathleen headed out together. They were in the port of Skagway only from 10 a.m. to 6:00 p.m. but that was plenty of time to connect with a poker game in a private room.

He wasn't doing well on the tables. Even the private cabin games that sprang up once gamblers identified members of their own tribe were failing him.

The night before he had connected with a couple of like-minded gentlemen at the poker table in the casino. They asked each other quietly, "Want to take this outside?" It didn't mean giving each other a bruising knuckle fight, but partaking in a civil private card game away from the casino and its tepid action.

"Are you in for the next hand?" asked one of the three who remained at the table. They were set up in the cabin suite of one of the players. Although cramped, the cabin with its table and four chairs accommodated their game space needs, and the room service accommodated their beverage needs.

Rupert preferred to keep a clear head when playing and was surprised that two of the players had each ordered a bottle of single malt scotch to start off the 11 a.m. game. One said he thought it brought him good luck and the other said he drank scotch at 11 a.m. and "What's it to you?" The bottle of the medicinal, seaweed taste of Laphrong sat next to the smoother Oban from the highlands. Less impressive were the two carafes, one of coffee for the third player and one of English Breakfast tea for Rupert. He had never managed to become accustomed to the bitter taste of the coffee bean.

Rupert mentally flipped through his available funds. He was ahead at this point. Should he continue or cash out? If only he knew the future.

Bloody hell, he thought. *If he knew the future he wouldn't be in this financial predicament.*

"Yes, deal me in." He refreshed his tea, sat and picked up his hand.

CHAPTER ELEVEN

"Not from that angle! Step off 15 feet further to my right." Sam shouted down from her dangling height on the rock face to the photographer 70 feet below.

This was the risk of recruiting a volunteer, she thought. James had immediately forgotten her instructions once her expensive digital camera was in his hands. He was no doubt enthusiastic and attempting to do his best. Perhaps he thought that a shot directly from below and between her legs would be artistic?

Muscles screaming, she stretched to the final handhold with her fingers, her right foot holding on precariously to her last position.

Artistic, perhaps. Flattering, not so much. Sam tightened her position in the harness and laughed when the movement swayed the lines. She bounced to regain her balance in the climbing gear.

There was something breathtaking about hanging on the side of a mountain with nothing but air about you and a few lines of rope holding you from certain injury and possible death. Some of the bravest, toughest men faltered when the moment came to trust their lives in the hands of strangers and a few pieces of rope.

Sam spread out her arms and leaned back into the harness, standing perpendicular to the rock face and parallel to the earth. She looked up to the treetops and surprisingly blue sky. For that moment, it was easy to believe that no cities existed, no other people existed. That she was alone in the universe with God.

Taking a deep breath, she began to bounce down the rock to the ground below, releasing line through the climbing gear to regulate her pace.

Once on the ground, she was disengaged from her climbing lines and jogged up the narrow, twisting path to the top of the 70-foot cliff. She listened carefully to the guide's instructions regarding the rapelling gear. This was not the time to be distracted from good advice!

Securing her lines into the rock anchors, she stood on the edge of the cliff. This was where a reasonable person would have a blinding flash of the obvious. You are about to step off a perfectly good mountain into air, supported by hooks that a teenage guide has anchored. You are further trusting that the ropes he has threaded through the rappelling gear are in the correct slots and all will be well.

She stepped off the mountain and walked down five feet. She looked down to James and gave him a signal to start taking shots. She would do the same rappel two more times to give the volunteer photographer ample opportunity to take photos from the top of the ledge where the head of the line began as she set her rappel, to lean over the mountain for shots of her from above, and now from below.

Sam leaned back into her harness and looked up to the blue sky, to the mountain on her far left and then to the far right at the granite rock face. She felt the solid vertical mass beneath her feet. One of the benefits of being a travel writer was the outrageous opportunities that presented themselves for her enjoyment and awe. Dangling seven stories above the forest floor was one of those moments and she was going to enjoy the ride.

Knowing full well her knees would pay dearly tomorrow for her exuberance and desire for the money shot today, she bounced off the rock, releasing a length of rope before pulling it back into the grip. She bounced down the remaining feet to the ground, feeling the gravitational pull to the rock in front of her and the earth below.

On terra firma after the last run, she repossessed her digital camera from her photographer-for-the-day. Sam took her own shots for her articles except when she herself was in the picture. She needed a picture of a climber popping off and away from the mountain and she couldn't ask a tourist to risk the knee stress for her shot.

The shots looked good and they would nicely balance out the article for OOTA. Rappelling and rock face climbing was definitely out of the ordinary. Although most cities had climbing walls, the judiciously placed foot and handgrips made climbing a physical, yet methodical feat. Climbing a rock face in the wild was about stretching to impossibly far spots where you hang by your finger nails while shifting your weight to the next possible spot, never totally sure that the next grip wasn't merely a figment of your imagination and only open air.

The usual adventures on a cruise to Alaska were not out of the ordinary. They were often staged events to capture the fascination of the tourists and create a Disney-esque experience of goldpanners and burly lumberjacks. But the readers of OOTA wanted more than staging; they wanted a unique and legitimate experience of the far north and the 49th state.

Alaska was an ideal place to push the physical boundaries of the average adventurer. Unlike some Central American countries where you may be taking your life into your hands by popping down a mountainside in borrowed gear and supported by unlicensed guides, Alaska offered the tourist the significant modern safety standards of the United States. OOTA travellers wanted a physical or cultural experience but a safe one, not one where only the mildest attention is paid to physical risk. There were few thrills that matched popping off the side of a mountain and then landing again on its vertical surface – especially when you knew that your ropes and harnesses were federally regulated.

In her photography class the day before, she had asked if anyone wanted to join her as her photographer for the day to take pictures of the task she was involved in and if she used any of the photos they shot, she would give the photography assistant full credit on the pages of OOTA. As she clicked through the digital photos that James had taken of her on the rock face, two stood out as being more than satisfactory for the story. James just may get a credit.

When she gave him the news about the shots, he high-fived her and immediately excused himself to text his friends.

As the adrenaline from the activity drained, Sam felt chilled. Noting the time, she grabbed her gear, crooked her finger at James and gave him a nod towards the waiting taxi. Although the cruise ship excursion would include transport to and from the location, Sam wanted to maximize her time on the mountain so had arranged a taxi to take them back to the ship as late as possible.

The gangway between the shore and ship turned several times between leaving solid land and resting on the floating Sea Wanderer. James and Sam were deep in conversation about careers in photography and whether he should choose more of his upcoming arts degree classes in that visual media. Making a blind turn, they stumbled into one of her dinner partners standing still on the gangway.

After mumbled apologies all around, Daniel turned back to his cell phone and continued his interrupted conversation. With a half-hearted wave, Sam and James continued towards the ship. Attempting not to eavesdrop, she none the less could not miss Daniel's deep voice hiss a whisper into his phone as she turned a corner, "Yes, I'll have the money soon. I'll take care of it!"

"Guess he has better cell connection there being we are so close to shore and everything. Seemed like a real intense kind of guy, eh?" Sam looked at James, unconsciously registering his laissez-faire approach to diction while her ear strained to hear more from Daniel. What the hell could he have been talking about? As Daniel turned the corner, she couldn't hear his next words but she read his lips. "I know - I only have seventeen days left."

Lip reading was a skill Sam had mastered with her younger sister Natasha who had been born deaf. Although her sister gained her hearing thanks to an experimental surgery in her early teens, Sam occasionally found use in the long-ago learned talent.

Daniel turned his head and Sam was blocked from seeing his lips. She continued towards the ship entry. Distracted by her bumbling encounter with Daniel, his barely controlled anger, and James' continuing conversation, Sam fumbled her boarding card and dropped it between the table and security podium.

The security officer waited patiently for Sam to get re-organized and hold her key card under the security scanner for the bar code to be read. "It is okay, ma'am. We know who you are, but we still need to scan you in. It is our protocol, to ensure we don't take off with anyone left ashore."

"Have you ever?"

"Left someone? Not very often but, unfortunately, it does occur. We can only delay in one location so long before we must move on to ensure timely arrival in the next port. It is our responsibility to ensure our passengers enjoy every single day of their cruise aboard the Sea Wanderer as well as our exceptional ashore opportunities. We hope you are enjoying your Sea Wanderer experience."

Sam almost expected the security officer to salute, so serious she was about her duties and promotional shtick. She didn't though; she just gave Sam and James another welcome aboard and stood aside for them to enter.

CHAPTER TWELVE

The ship had pulled away from the port of Skagway and the sisters had gone to their respective cabins to unload their purchases and change before attending a presentation on the formation and calving of glaciers.

Lauren gave a quick rap on her sister's stateroom door and then called out.

"Kathleen, it's Lauren. Before we go to the presentation, I want to talk about that article Sam might do on the Corey Art Project. Well not on the project, per se, but the inclusion of the project. It will be brilliant for fundraising."

She rapped again and then paused, "Kathleen, I am tired of talking through the door. Can you open up?"

After the twins had disembarked from the Sea Wanderer with several thousand other passengers, they spent half an hour perusing the souvenir and jewellery shops that frequent most cruise ship destinations. After each purchasing a warm jacket embroidered with the word 'Alaska' on the front, they met their tour bus and boarded with a boisterous group of fellow travellers.

Skagway is at the northern tip of the Inside Passage and is the historical heart of the Klondike Gold Rush. Its deep port was the gateway to the gold fields and the town had been the beginning of many a gold searcher's journey. From this point, prospectors gripped by gold fever had ascended the Chilkoot and White Pass in search of wealth. The gold rush mania the prospectors created made Skagway an instant city and, at the time, the largest one in Alaska.

After their city tour and a walk along the historic streets, Kathleen and Lauren made their way back to the ship.

Kathleen opened the door, pulled her sister inside quickly, closed the cabin door and leaned against it. "I want to talk to you too. But not about Sam. About these."

Kathleen took off her sweater and showed her arms to Lauren, still bruised where Daniel had held her so roughly.

"What the hell. Where did you get these? Is this Daniel's doing? Wait till I get a hold of him. I am going to rip him a new one. I am going to scratch out his eyeballs. I am going to leave serious, serious marks. Where is he?" Lauren had a feral gleam in her eye as she stalked around the small square footage of the stateroom, as if she could magically make her brother-in-law appear.

"Calm down, Lauren. You are not going to confront Daniel."

"What?" Lauren spun around and looked at her sister.

"Daniel is not going to change because you want him to. He certainly isn't going to change because I want him to. He wants me to do what he wants me to do when he wants me to do it and how he wants me to do it. He has mortgaged the condo and I think his firm is in trouble." Kathleen rubbed her hands over her face, as if to remove the pain.

"I don't know who he even is anymore. Yes, he gave us this cruise out of the blue, but I think it was more to keep an eye on me than to give me pleasure. He keeps pushing me to let him handle the brokerage account and the other investments. But I don't trust him anymore. With the money. With me. He asks me every day to invite him into a more active role in the organization. I even found papers he brought on board for me to sign over the investing authority."

Lauren nodded. "Rupert has been asking me to think about it, too. Suggesting that Daniel could make us real money from the millions and then we wouldn't have to be so concerned about fundraising for the Corey Art Project. But I don't like it. It's one thing to play fast and loose with his and his client's money, but we can't let Daniel play fast and loose with ours. It's against everything mom and dad wanted. This isn't our money; we are only stewards of it." Lauren paced around the tiny cabin – three feet in one direction, turned around, and paced back three.

"Kathleen, why don't you just leave him?" she whispered.

"I tried. When I asked him for a separation, he shook me so hard I thought my teeth would come loose. That's when he left these marks." She said, covering up her arms once more with her sweater.

"When he came up with this cruise idea, I knew there was something more to it than just a trip. It is a waste of his time, and the internet and mobile connections must be making him insane.

"I want to get out but he isn't going to let me go easily. I feel like I am being watched. He questions me every time I am away from him unless I am at the office. He seems to know where I am all the time. I was going to disable the GPS tracking on my IPhone but he would know that I had done so and would question why. I purchased a silver sleeve instead and it blocks my location." She slid her mobile into the radio frequency blocking device and showed it to Lauren. "It's called a Silent Pocket."

Lauren looked at Kathleen and sighed. "He is an asshole. He is even a greedy, self-serving asshole. But is all this cloak and dagger business really necessary?"

Kathleen opened the closet and pulled a file folder out of the bottom of Daniel's bag. She handed it to Lauren.

"Shit shit shit!" Lauren whispered, looking at each document.

"My thoughts exactly," said Kathleen.

The two sisters came together in a tight hug, unhampered by the file folder in Lauren's hand. For several moments the sisters held on to each other tightly, regretfully letting go. Kathleen pulled away first, wiping the dampness from below her eyes.

Lauren looked once more at the copy of Kathleen's will and life insurance policy in the file before handling it back to her sister.

"Put it back where he left it."

CHAPTER THIRTEEN

Dinner after a day ashore was often livelier than a day at sea. Passengers had their tall tales to share from their day, along with complaints about excursion queues and re-boarding crushes.

After Sam described her day up in the air, clinging to the mountain, Kathleen and Lauren shared their impressions of the Aboriginal art they had seen in different shops that day. After discussing the possibilities of incorporating totem art into the Art Project, the dinner table conversation turned naturally to Lauren's excitement over Sam's article idea on the Corey Art Project.

"So if the article highlighted the needs of the project, we may get some new and significant sponsors," Lauren summarized her earlier conversation with Sam to Daniel, Rupert, Kathleen and George.

"How does the foundation sponsorship work now?" Sam asked Lauren.

"We receive sponsorship and donations to the Corey Art Project through its charitable status. But most of the revenue is from a sort of family trust. We also call them the 'millions' in jest. That was the word my father had for the lottery money," Lauren laughed.

"The money Kathleen and I inherited is separate from the Corey Art Project charity. We donate the yearly investment revenue made on the principal. Both Aunt Jennifer and our parents believed that it was important that we keep control over the money we donate and how it is invested, versus a foundation board."

"Do you pay yourself first and then donate, or does the foundation pay your salaries?" asked Sam, ignoring the first rule of cruise ship dinner conversation: avoid topics of money, careers and wealth.

"All the money that is derived from interest, dividends and what have you goes directly to the Art Project. We both receive very good salaries, indexed for inflation. We also have a well-funded pension plan," Kathleen responded.

"So, technically, you could withdraw funding for the Corey Art Project from your sources anytime?" asked Sam.

"Technically, yes. But if the Corey Art Project ceased to exist we would find another project or charity that would be what Aunt Jennifer had in mind. Besides, we have an obligation to our aunt and parents. It was their dream and now it is ours," said Kathleen. She looked directly at Daniel. "Nor would we risk the funds in risky ventures or speculative investments."

Sam watched as Daniel moved his eyes from Kathleen to Rupert. The two men looked at each other for a long second and then away to their plates. Everyone was quiet. *That amount of money could certainly create problems in family,* Sam thought. *No one knew that more than she.*

Sam turned to George and made an effort to change the conversation to a lighter vein. "How was your day George?"

"Well it started out like shit!" That caught everyone's attention.

"I was going from the dock to the fishing boat – and well if I didn't miss my footing and step between the boat and the dock. Whoosh – wetter than the Coho salmon I was supposed to be fishing for. I had to come back and change and damn it if I didn't miss my tour – and I was looking forward to reeling in a couple big ones. Damn it anyways."

Well that was a good diversion, Sam smiled.

Day Four

Ashore in Juneau and aboard the ship Sea Wanderer

Stuffed Chicken Breast with Wild Mushrooms, Figs and Stilton

Or

Grilled Swordfish Steak, Roasted New Potatoes, Ragout of Baby Vegetables

Or

Penne Pasta with Smoked Salmon, Belvedere Vodka and Dill Cream

CHAPTER FOURTEEN

Sam followed the winding snake of passengers disembarking from the Sea Wanderer to the town of Juneau. Looking far ahead, she could see Kathleen's French twist and Lauren's swinging blond curtain. The blondes were wearing the Alaska jackets they had bought in a port shop in Skagway, one in navy with ivory lining and a blue scarf and the other an ivory jacket with navy lining and a pink scarf.

Good choice, thought Sam. The windbreakers with reversible fleece linings were warm and waterproof. Although it was June, it was Alaska and many people find themselves underdressed for the cool breezes and misty weather.

Sam looked around at the many people in the snaking queue that stretched between her and the sisters. Too far away to wave or call out, Sam contented herself in knowing that she would see them at dinner that evening.

Juneau is the only American state capital that cannot be

reached by road from anywhere else in Alaska. It is cut off by mountains, water, forest and ice. Sam's goal for the day was to photograph one of Alaska's most accessible ice faces and barriers to the outside world. The Mendenhall Glacier.

The ashore excursion included a visit to the glacier and then perhaps to the glacier gardens or salmon bake, depending on how long she was at the glacier. Any excursion that also included food was a temptation, but Sam felt an obligation to OOTA to write as many relevant articles as possible on the cruise. "The glacier and gardens it is," she decided.

Sam was pleasantly surprised to see the twins on the bus to the glacier.

"Sam! We didn't know you would be on this tour! How far are you going?"

Lauren was referring to the choices of the .3 mile Creek Trail, which took 20 minutes, the .5 mile Steep Creek Trail which involved an hour of your time or the more adventurous 3.5 mile Eastern Glacier loop which followed the glacial trim line for two gruelling hours.

"I want to fit in the Glacier Gardens so I think the Steep Creek Trail option would be plenty. Also there is a better chance of bugs, bears and sunburn on the Eastern Glacier Loop. How about you? Which are you choosing?"

The two sisters looked at each other for a long moment as if still deciding their plan for the day. Kathleen spoke up first, which was rare for the twins. "After the Steep Creek Trail, I am off to the Glacier Gardens for an hour of botanical bliss. Lauren is heading back to town to visit St. Nicholas Russian Orthodox Church."

"Oh that sounds interesting as well. What attracts you to the church?"

"It is unique in many ways," Lauren replied. "One is that it is small, in the shape of an octagon, so small that everyone stands during a service.

"I hope the service isn't too long then," Sam laughed.

"According to my research, the church was built in 1893 by local Tlingits. At the time there was considerable pressure for them to convert to Christianity and by joining this denomination they could continue to speak their native language in the church. A priest by the name of Veniaminov had translated the Bible into Tlingit in the mid-1800s. Even today services are held in Tlingit.

"As well, the Sam McClain Watercolours are housed there. He painted watercolours of orthodox churches in the 1960s and 1970s. Since early 2011, the collection has been housed there. Would you like to join me in exploring?"

Sam thought about the interesting shots she could take of the church and whether there may be a story as well. She turned to Lauren's sister, "Sorry Kathleen, St. Nicholas has won me over the gardens." The sisters looked at each other and smiled.

An hour later, the three women stopped at the US Forest Service visitor centre and found a ranger to answer the many questions they had about the glacier, the geology of Mendenhall Lake and even bears playing with salmon.

Satisfied, Sam and Lauren saw Kathleen off in a taxi to the Glacier Gardens and then boarded the Mendenhall Glacier Express, a bus that took them back to the dockside.

"Should we take a cab to the church or are you up to another walk?" asked Lauren.

"I think it is only five blocks according to the map so I am up to it if you are," responded Sam.

They navigated the throng of tourists and climbed South Franklin past Ferry and Front, where Sam paused outside the Hearthside bookstore, tempted to go in. Lauren pulled her away and they continued past 2nd, 3rd and 4th. Although it was only a half dozen blocks on the map, the uphill climb had the two women puffing when they arrived at the church between 5th and 6th.

"Is it under construction, do you think?" Lauren asked. There were open boards revealing the foundation and tarps hung around the entrance. The two women walked to a display board at the front of the property.

Although the church was a historic landmark and a testament to the Tlingit and Orthodox peoples, the building was in trouble. The weather of Alaska had not been kind to St. Nicholas. When it was reroofed in 2007, the supports for the bell tower were found to be rotten. The church was not secured to its foundation and was slipping off in some places. To add to these issues, the church was on a hill and water draining under the building was adding to moisture concerns for the foundation.

The small but active St. Nicholas parish was teaming up with ROSSIA, the Russian Orthodox Sacred Sites in Alaska, to preserve the historic Orthodox Church. The building needed help in maintenance and reconstruction.

"Let's go in," Lauren whispered.

Luckily the priest was in the building and gave them a tour of the 18th century iconography and further history of the church. In 1892, 700 of the 1500 Aboriginal people in the community were baptized in the Orthodox faith. The church stands today as the oldest, continually used church in southeast Alaska.

Before the two women walked downhill to the ship, Sam

asked Lauren for a few minutes alone. She sat in the church and prayed. For herself and for the family she no longer saw.

CHAPTER FIFTEEN

Standing in line outside the formal dining room, Sam smoothed down the simple black dinner dress that was her most used evening attire. Her old friend was made from a wrinkle free fabric, which was the essential characteristic of all of her clothing.

Can it be washed, hung to dry, rolled up in her one travelling suitcase and come out looking fabulous at the other end? That was the criteria for clothes for the professional traveller. As she was on the road for weeks at a time between breaks with friends who had laundry equipment, Sam needed clothing that could be laundered en route and a packing style to maximize items in her one bag.

Sam had browsed the posted dinner menu as soon as she came back on the ship. *Grilled Swordfish Steak and Roasted New Potatoes. Or Penne Pasta with Salmon and what-cha-ma-call-it sauce.* The walk from the dockside to the church this afternoon justified a quick glance at the dessert list. *Crème Brule Cheesecake.*

Keeping her size down to a ten was a constant struggle with the wonderful food that often accompanied the locations where she travelled. Luckily her days often included walking and climbing. When she felt she was losing the battle of the svelte, she put in extra time at the closest gym. But tonight, after the walk at the glacier and the climb to the church, she felt justified in choosing between the Crème Brule cheesecake and the dark chocolate mousse. Maybe she should have both.

"Well hello there, Sam!" Sam turned her head to see the buoyant George walking down the perpendicular path to the dining queue. His arm was in a sling and he was without his customary tie and jacket.

"George, what happened?" Sam was beginning to suspect that George was either the unluckiest or the clumsiest person she had ever met.

"Well, I was heading to the area where we get off the ship and damn if I didn't trip on my own feet going down the stairs between decks and wrench my shoulder. It has caused me trouble over the years so it doesn't surprise me that this would be the thing to go. "

"Did you get to see any of Juneau?"

"I was headed out to see the humpback whales, sea lions and other wildlife. At least that is what they promised in the ashore excursion brochure. But I missed all that while I was down in the medical clinic. I did get off for an hour or so before we left port. I ran into one of the sisters in the gangway. I can't tell them apart to be honest. She was a bit in a flap herself."

"Let me help you – was her hair up or down?"

"Well she was doing that fluffy thingy you girls do with your hair."

"Fluffy thing?"

George touched his one hand to his bald head and then waved his hand about. "Like that."

Still confused, Sam tried. "Was she wearing a navy or ivory jacket?"

"Well it was kind of inside out she was struggling with it and her scarf at the same time."

"Aha. What colour was the scarf?" Sam jumped on the one detail that would answer their question

"Now, that I don't remember. I used to be very detail oriented. But I was under the influence of codeine."

Sam and George were at the front of the line and found their table without further mishap. Lauren, Daniel and Rupert followed shortly.

Lauren sat beside George and leaned in sympathetically. "Oh George, what happened now?"

"Well, it was foolishness really. Tripped. Wrenched shoulder. Missed the ashore."

"George and I were trying to figure out which of you two, you or Kathleen, he met in the gangway earlier."

"Well, we didn't actually meet," George clarified. "I just noticed one of you as I was walking by in the other direction."

Lauren pursed her lips, tilting her head to one side. "Well George, I don't remember seeing you. It is possible that it could have been either of us."

"Their likeness is disturbing, isn't it?" Rupert added. "When I first met Kathleen after dating Lauren for a couple of weeks, I was discombobulated. They are remarkably similar. It is splendid that they at least dress differently to help me along."

"You don't mix me up with my sister," chided Lauren with a laugh, poking him in the shoulder with her index finger.

"Not now that I love you and know every small line around your eyes," he joked back.

"I don't have lines around my eyes!"

Rupert picked up Lauren's hand that was now resting on his arm and gave it a quick kiss. "Only when you laugh, my love."

Across the table, Daniel harrumphed.

"Where is Kathleen? Is she on her way?" Sam asked Daniel.

Studying the menu, Daniel thought of the note that the cabin steward had passed him not an hour before. "She wanted some alone time. She is quite an introvert and sometimes she finds so many people and activities overwhelming."

"That's too bad," replied George. "She's good company. Hopefully tomorrow then."

Rupert mused. "I find that one of the interesting things about the twins, George. Kathleen is an introvert, Lauren an extrovert. Kathleen is thinking a wonderful week alone with my husband on board a ship. Lauren is thinking about the two thousand people she would like to meet and make friends with!"

Sam looked again at Daniel. "I last saw her when she took a taxi to the Glacier Gardens. She seemed in a good frame of mind then. How about you, Lauren? Did you see her after you and I separated after we saw the church?" Lauren had told Sam she wanted to shop more before embarking, so Sam had gone ahead to the gangway before her.

"No, I last saw her when she got into the cab at the glacier." Lauren looked at Daniel. "She will be fine, though?"

Daniel was now looking at the wine list. "I expect so."

Turning to Lauren, he pronounced, "Lauren said to tell you

not to worry. She just needs a few hours to herself."

I hope she is thinking about those transfer papers, he thought. He had spent the afternoon playing poker with Rupert and a couple of other men he had met in the pub. He had won the pot and the few thousand dollars were a nice boost to his morale, but nowhere near the funds he needed to surrender to the boys in seventeen days. Rupert, on the other hand, was in a surprisingly good mood even though he had lost his stake. That Rupert, in spite of his upcoming possible unemployment and gambling debts, managed to find the sunny side of life was beyond irritating. *Damn him.*

Sam asked George if he needed any assistance managing the multi-part menu, one wing down as he was.

"No, I always just listen to the recommendations from the waiter and chose from that. It seems the print on the menu is too small. I have trouble focusing on the letters."

Sam settled on the *Penne Pasta with Smoked Salmon, Belvedere Vodka and Dill Cream,* confident in a enjoying a delicious meal with her unique tablemates.

Day Five

Aboard the Ship Sea Wanderer and ashore in Juneau

Fillet of Halibut and Basil Risotto

Or

*Roast Gressingham Duck,
Apple and Cranberry Savoury Stuffing*

Or

*Braised Prime Beef Short Ribs
in Merlot Wine Sauce
with Whipped Potatoes*

CHAPTER SIXTEEN

It was 2 a.m.

Daniel grabbed the lapels of the jacket worn by the Captain of the Sea Wanderer and shook the garment and the man wearing it. His eyes bored into the Captain's.

"My wife is on the ship. My wife is not on the ship. Which is it, Captain? Where exactly is my wife?"

The Captain stepped back, pulling his uniform jacket free from Daniel's grip. He smoothed his lapels with his palms and took a notebook from his inside pocket.

"According to our security personnel, she disembarked yesterday morning at 1000 hours and re-boarded yesterday at 1500 hours. You made us aware of her disappearance at 2200 last evening." The captain returned the notebook to his inside pocket.

Taking a deep breath, he looked the other man directly in the eyes, and said quietly, "Since that time, we have searched extensively for her in every area of the ship. She simply seems to have vanished."

When dinner was finished the evening before, Daniel and Rupert had returned to the pub for a couple of after dinner drinks. Lauren had begged off to her cabin, saying it was a long day and she had walked more than any reasonable person should in a day.

When Daniel wandered back to the cabin, it looked unchanged from when he had changed for dinner. In other words, no Kathleen.

He checked the safe. Her passport was folded on top of his. He relocked the safe and began to search the room.

He opened the drawers to the left of the built-in desk and found her wallet on top of her underwear. Inside was American and Canadian cash, her two credit cards and her key card for the room. He went to the door, stepped out and closed the door. He tried the card in the electronic bar on the door and opened the door to the cabin following the brief green acceptance flash.

Stepping two feet to the left, he knocked on the door of the cabin next door. Rupert had just gone in and he answered the door fully dressed minus his tie.

"Yes, Daniel? Another whisky, perhaps?" Rupert whispered.

"No, just looking for Kathleen. Is she in there with Lauren?"

"No, and Lauren is fast asleep."

"Wake her and ask her if she has seen Kathleen."

"I will not. Kathleen might have just gone out for a drink herself."

"Wake her up. I need to know."

"Bloody hell, Daniel. Fine. Fine." Turning away from the door, he walked to his wife and shook her shoulder lightly.

"Lauren, darling. Wake up. Do you know where Kathleen is?

She is not in her cabin."

Lauren gave her head a shake, clearing her thoughts. What had he asked exactly?

"Are you asking if I have seen Kathleen tonight?"

Daniel spoke from the open door through clenched teeth. "That is exactly what I am asking. Do you know where she is?"

"I said, I haven't seen her since I left the Mendenhall Glacier. Do you want me to get dressed and look with you? Three of us could search faster than you alone."

"Yes, yes, but hurry." Daniel made a scooping motion with his hand as if he could move Lauren out of bed himself and into the corridor to begin the search. Rupert held out a robe for Lauren. She moved from the bed into the arms of the garment and knotted the belt.

"I'll get dressed and start with the medical center, then the library, and the art gallery. Rupert, you go to the coffee shop, the buffet, and the pub. Daniel, you go to the disco, the casino, the champagne bar and the observation deck. Back here in half an hour."

Half an hour later, the three were back in the cabin. "I need to call security," Daniel said. Privately, he thought, *If only she had signed the papers.*

CHAPTER SEVENTEEN

Sam had been awakened by Rupert banging on her door at 5 a.m.

"What! What! What!" the rumpled, pajama-wearing Sam shouted, opening the door in a rush. She had been having a delicious dream of a magical Crème Brule that was made with full cream but mysteriously carried zero calories.

"Have you seen Kathleen? We can't seem to find her anywhere?" Rupert breathed, holding his chest like he had been running.

"What do you mean you can't find her?"

"No. One. Can. Find. Her," said Rupert slowly, emphasizing each word, as if the English words themselves were the problem with Sam's comprehension.

"We will be in Ketchikan in four or five hours and we will contact the police there," Rupert breathed, holding his chest.

"Come in here and sit down. It looks like you are having a

heart attack."

Sam pulled Rupert into her cabin and pushed him into the only chair.

"First let me get you a glass of water. Now start from the beginning and speak slowly."

Gulping the water, Rupert put the empty glass down on the table. "Lauren is in shock. She must be. She isn't frantic or pacing, which is her usual way of dealing with stress. She is strangely calm. Daniel is running around like a madman. And I, well I am just running period. Trying to think of all the places that she might be. Security will ask all the stewards to do a room-to-room search at 8 a.m.

"But what if someone has her in their cabin and is doing God knows what with her?" Rupert started to hyperventilate. Sam pushed his head between his knees.

"Just breathe Rupert, just breathe."

"I can't help but think whatever happened could have happened to Lauren. Oh, God," Rupert moaned from his hunched position.

"But it didn't and we don't know if anything sinister has happened to Kathleen either," added Sam.

"I don't know what to do. The last time we saw her it was in Juneau. Do we go back there? You can't drive there, so we would have to take the Alaska Marine Highway, which really is a ferry and why they call it a highway is beyond me. That is very confusing. Don't you think that is very confusing?

"And the girls were just planning their annual trip to celebrate their parents' wedding anniversary. I think it was New Orleans this year. Now that might not happen. Lauren will be heart broken. Well she will be more heartbroken if Kathleen is hurt or God forbid worse," Rupert continued, his breathing laboured and speech racing.

"Rupert, breathe."

"Or should we stay on the ship until we get to Vancouver? I am usually more decisive with these matters. I am the calm one in my family, the logical one. Well, I used to be."

"Oh bollocks," Sam said, using one of Rupert's own favourite British curses. "You are just worried. Now pull yourself together and get back to your wife before she thinks we are having a torrid affair."

That brought Rupert to ground, as he lifted his head quickly and looked her directly in the eye, squinting his own. "If you think that I would ever...."

"No," she interrupted, "You wouldn't, Rupert, but I am glad to see you are getting your colour back." Sam patted his cheek and pushed him towards the door. "Now get out of here so I can dress and see if I can help in any way."

Sam shut the door on Rupert and then removed her notebook from her pull case. She wrote down everything that she remembered of the day before, including facts, thoughts, and comments of others. This may become a police investigation and unfortunately not only did Sam know what that involved, she had been in the eye of the storm before. Once that happened, stress took over and little details were lost. Details that might save a life.

Fifteen minutes later, a dressed Sam went to find Lauren. *How was she holding up?* she wondered.

A missing family member? Sam knew exactly how Lauren was holding up. She wouldn't be holding up – not at all.

CHAPTER EIGHTEEN

Sam turned down the passageway that led to Rupert and Lauren's cabin and was brought up short by the two of them plus Daniel walking in the opposite direction.

"We have been asked to go to the disco to meet with security and provide information," Rupert said. "You should come with us."

As they entered the elevator to take them to Deck Six, Lauren consoled Rupert, "I just know if Kathleen was in danger or if she was hurt, I would feel it. We are very intuitive with each other. I don't feel any anxiety from her. Not like I have over the past several weeks."

Daniel looked sharply at Lauren and then away.

The disco was not open to the public at 5:30 a.m. and the full house lights were up. The room was brightly lit and the glass balls and other shiny décor that looked so magical in the evening looked merely gaudy in the full light. Two officers were sitting at a table with a laptop computer, reviewing security records. Although they were neatly attired, Sam couldn't help but think that were looking a little tired as well. No one in the room, probably, had slept much the night before.

One of the officers looked up and greeted them with a sympathetic but sobering look. He introduced himself as Officer Burns and his fellow officer as Officer Seger. He asked them to sit down around the table.

"At this point in time we are uncertain as to whether Mrs. Zachery is aboard or not, has been the victim of foul play or not, has fallen overboard or chosen to leave the ship willingly. I am sure that you can appreciate that we wish to resolve this issue quickly and quietly for all concerned."

"Bad press you mean!" Daniel interrupted.

"If you are referring to our last season of Norwalk virus and the deaths that occurred on this vessel, yes, Mr. Zachery, our public image is of importance to our company and our senior officers." Officer Burns spoke with a firm, calm voice. "However, there are other issues to consider. We don't want other passengers to become panicked or go off half-cocked on a search and rescue mission."

"What about the police?" asked Sam.

"Once we determine that Mrs. Zackery is not on the boat, then we will endeavour to understand whether she left the boat willingly and when and where. Then, we discuss next steps with other security forces. Our first step is this one, interviewing each of you to maximize our information so we can create the best reflection of her day yesterday."

"I will be sitting over there," he pointed to a table twenty feet away. "One by one, could you come over and join me? You first,

Mr. Zackery."

Daniel stood up and joined the officer at the second table.

"I have your full name as Daniel Richard Zackery. That is correct, sir?"

"Of course it is, you have a copy of my passport right there on your screen."

The officer moved the laptop computer to shield the monitor screen from Daniel's view. "Just trying to do my job here, Mr. Zackery and locate Mrs. Zackery as quickly as possible."

Daniel nodded.

"You joined the cruise in Vancouver five days ago and the last time you saw your wife was...?"

"Yesterday morning when she left with her sister to go ashore for an excursion."

"You didn't go with her ashore?"

"Ashores aren't my thing. She would enjoy herself more with her sister than with me, especially viewing botanical gardens and native art."

"You mentioned last night to your table mates that she had told you that she wasn't joining the group for dinner. Did she tell you that when she left in the morning?"

"No, she left me a note and the cabin steward gave it to me when I came to the cabin around 5 p.m."

"Do you know when the steward received the note?"

"No, I assumed that it was earlier and she wanted to ensure that I received it versus leaving it in the cabin where it may be overlooked. I don't really know why she left it with the steward. She could have called me. She knows I have my cell phone with me, even though it costs a fortune to use it aboard the ship."

"Yes, internet and cellular are a bit pricy aboard, I would

agree. But we are a moving vessel, sir, dependent on satellite technology" said Burns.

Daniel almost found himself in a debate with the security officer about the pricing of their services, when he caught himself. He needed this person to see him as cooperative.

"We will check with the steward regarding the note," said the officer, writing a note to himself on the yellow notepad on the table.

"Has your wife been demonstrating any depression or confusion recently?"

"Do you mean could she have thrown herself overboard?" Daniel asked bluntly.

"Mr. Zackery, our video surveillance and computer identification system shows your wife leaving the ship using her ship identification card and coming back to the ship several hours later. She re-boarded at a particularly busy time so no officer has been able to definitively say he saw her. One security officer thinks he saw Mrs. Zackery re-board, but even he is not exactly certain.

"No one has actually spoken to her since yesterday morning when she was last seen at the Mendenhall Glacier. We must think of all the possibilities. But there is no need to borrow trouble, as my grandmother would say, and there are many areas on this ship where a person could lose themselves," the officer finished wryly.

"But, does that mean she is hiding? Someone took her somewhere on the ship? It doesn't make any sense."

"We'll get to the bottom of it all, Mr. Zackery. Now perhaps you can answer a few more personal questions."

"Go ahead."

"Is your wife a woman of financial means? Who would her estate go to upon her death? Does she have life insurance? For how much and who is the beneficiary?"

"Are you asking if I killed my wife, officer?" Daniel said quietly.

"No, I am not, Mr. Zackery. I am asking pertinent questions that may or may not assist us in understanding the alleged disappearance of Mrs. Zackery."

"My wife manages sort of a family trust fund over which she and her sister have complete control. It is estimated to be worth about $80 million. If she died, her sister, Lauren, would have complete control. If Kathleen and I divorced, our marital contract would come into force."

"Marital contract?"

"It is like a prenup in the United States."

"And it reads...," asked the officer.

"None of the assets previously under Kathleen's parent's control are assets to be divided. Neither Rupert nor I can receive any of the 'millions,' as we call the funds, in a divorce settlement."

"And if both women become deceased, where do these infamous millions go?"

"Through lawyers, a trust would be created with the revenues supporting charitable works, just as the two sisters are running it now."

"And life insurance?"

"My wife has a life insurance policy for $5 million as do I. We are each other's beneficiaries." Daniel answered, reluctantly.

"Just one last question Mr. Zachery and then I will talk to you sister-in-law and brother-in-law. Had you met George Simpson or Samantha Anderson before your voyage?"

"My table mates? No."

"Thank you, Mr. Zackery. Please ask your sister-in-law to join me."

CHAPTER NINETEEN

"Mrs. Williams, I am sorry that you are finding yourself in this situation. We will do everything we can to ensure that your sister is found quickly and found safely. Now can you tell me about your day yesterday?"

Lauren told the officer about joining Kathleen and leaving the ship, meeting up with Sam along the way, and their adventures on the trail at the Mendenhall Glacier. "Then, Sam and I saw Kathleen off in a taxi to the Glacier Gardens. We went on our way to see the church, then came back down to a bar, had a drink and then separated at the dock."

"You walked to and from the church?"

"Yes, the little Orthodox one – St. Nicholas."

"And then?"

"We walked back down towards the pier looking into the shops on South Franklin Street. We kept walking until we passed all the tourist stops and went into a restaurant and bar on the waterfront."

"Do you remember the name?"

"Yes, it was called Twisted Fish – how can you forget a name like that?"

"Do you remember anyone who served you?"

"Yes, we were sitting at the bar. The bartender's name was Scottie. Kind of cute with a dark beard and moustache. Originally from the southern states, he said. One of those guys who wanted to live out his boyhood fantasy of living in the wilderness."

"Not a fan of the wilderness, Mrs. Williams?"

"No, my idea of roughing it is no room service."

Burns held back a smile. The sister was holding up well, considering her sister was missing. "After the stop at Twisted Fish, where did you go?"

"Sam and I walked to the dock where we separated."

"Why was that?"

"What?"

"That you and Sam Anderson separated at the dock?"

"I believe she wanted to shop a little longer and I was ready to call it a day."

"Mrs. Zackery took a taxi, you say? What colour was it?"

"Yellow I think. Why does that matter?"

The officer looked at his notepad. "Juneau Taxi has yellow cabs and is the largest fleet. There is also EverGreen Taxi, Capital Cab and Taku Taxi. This will help us narrow down which one to call to find out where she took the taxi to."

"But didn't she go to the Glacier Gardens?" Lauren asked haltingly.

"That is what she said to you and Ms. Anderson, you are correct."

Lauren realized then that the officer wasn't going to take her word or any other person's for what had occurred the day and evening before.

"Tell me, Mrs. Williams about... where is it...?" he shuffled his papers back to the top copy of notes. "Oh yes, here it is... I believe your brother-in-law called it a family trust."

"The money is from my aunt who won it in a lotto. My father and mother were custodians of the money and upon their deaths, my sister and I inherited the obligation."

"Obligation?"

"Yes, it is our obligation to use the funds generated from the trust to fulfill my aunt's desire to help children at risk, to set them on the right path as it were. We put the investment revenue from the funds into a charity called the Corey Art Project. This is the same project my aunt began and my parents ran. Kathleen and I have been wholly responsible for several years now both for the trust and the Corey Art Project."

"So if she passed away, what would happen to the art project as you call it and the trust fund?"

"Don't ask that." Lauren whispered.

"I have to ask, Mrs. Williams."

"I would have to run it by myself," whispered Lauren, looking down at her hands. "I don't know if I could do that. Rupert could help me but it wouldn't be the same."

"You can spend the money in the trust as you please, is that not the case?"

"Well, the investment revenue goes to the Corey Art Project."

"Yes, but do not you and your sister, and if your sister was deceased, you alone, have total control over the principal and investment revenue."

"Yes, but control is not ownership."

"I don't understand, Mrs. Williams."

Lauren looked at the officer. The millions weren't hers or Kathleen's, any more than they were her parents when they were alive. Each generation were only stewards of what their aunt had been blessed with.

Lauren was also aware that wealth came not only with privilege but challenges. Her aunt had quickly found that too much money could lead to false friends and a life of dissolution. Five years after winning the lottery, Jennifer Corey had begun the pseudo trust fund, pulled herself out of depression brought on by a feeling of low self-worth in her unearned wealth, put herself on an annual salary and started to work for the good of her community. The depression lifted. She found herself surrounded by those with like-minded goals for the at-risk youth of the city. She was no longer the party girl and had set her mind to more serious matters.

Lauren knew her aunt's story well. Aunt Jennifer had shared it with the twins to ensure that they didn't fall down the same hole into which she had. After the twins inherited from their parents, they spent time researching the impact of fast, unearned wealth. Although contrary to expectations, undeserved wealth led lottery winners to be less concerned about the plight of those less fortunate. Lottery winners were also disproportionately likely to go bankrupt. These findings only ensured that the twins were more committed to their aunt's and parent's plans.

"No officer, apparently you don't."

"One last question, had you ever met Samantha Anderson or George Simpson before this cruise?"

"No, I hadn't."

"Could you please ask your husband to join me?"

CHAPTER TWENTY

Rupert had been watching Officer Burns interview Lauren and he itched to be beside her to support her. Once or twice when he had risen to join her, Officer Seger had laid his hand on Rupert's arm and shook his head. It was clear that the officer expected Lauren to present her facts alone.

When she stood up and walked over to his chair, he stood and gave her an embrace. "Are you all right?"

"No, but I'm not worried. Except for this circus. I know that Kathleen is fine. We will eventually find out exactly what happened."

"I hope you are correct," he mumbled against her hair. But privately he thought she was in denial of the outcome of the events of the past day.

Lauren patted her husband's cheeks and pulled from the embrace. "He wants to talk to you now."

"I don't know what I can add to whatever you and Daniel had

to say. I didn't even see her yesterday."

"Go on," she encouraged.

Rupert took the seat that his wife had vacated a moment earlier and told the officer, "I didn't even see her yesterday."

"That is what you said earlier."

"Because it is the truth."

"As you say, sir. Now, a couple of questions and you can take your wife to your cabin. She seems tuckered out."

Rupert looked at Lauren. Surprisingly, except for the last few minutes, she had been remarkably positive about Kathleen's disappearance. Only now she sat, her hands in her lap, looking at her fingers as if they were foreign objects.

"Now, a few questions. Have you ever met Samantha Anderson or George Simpson before this cruise?"

"Who is Samantha Anderson?"

"Your dinner table mate?"

"Oh Sam! No, not before this cruise."

"What would happen to the trust fund if Kathleen Zackery died?"

"It would go to Lauren to control."

"And own."

"Yes technically."

"And if your wife Lauren died, what would happen to the trust fund?"

Rupert jumped out of the chair, the movement toppling the chair to the floor. "What the hell are you saying?"

"Nothing, I am merely asking questions."

"No, you are not," Rupert's voice rising. "You are saying I killed Kathleen. That I would do that to my wife." He looked back to the table where Sam, Lauren and Daniel sat.

Daniel jumped up. "If you did do this, tell me where she is! Where is her body?"

Rupert ran to Lauren and grabbed her two hands from her lap. "Look at me Lauren. I. Did. Not. Do. This."

"I know," she whispered. *This is so much more awful than I thought*, she thought.

She shook her head. Thinking that she wasn't convinced, Rupert dropped her hands and then he walked out of the room.

"Well, hello everyone." George entered the disco. "What's going on? I was asked to report here about a missing person."

Lauren looked at George, then back to Sam. She did not look at Daniel. She left.

CHAPTER TWENTY-ONE

The two officers looked up at George. Officer Seger asked if he was George Simpson.

Officer Burns asked Sam to join him at his table, ignoring the chair that Rupert had overturned in his agitation.

He turned to Daniel. "Mr. Zackery," he said, "we will be interviewing Ms. Anderson and Mr. Simpson and then reporting back to the Captain. He will report to you any findings that he believes are pertinent. You are free to go."

"I want to talk to him as soon as you report to him," Daniel said standing in front of Officer Burns, his arms folded across his chest.

"That will be up to the Captain, Mr. Zachery. But we will make him aware of your request."

Daniel uncrossed his arms and stalked out of the disco.

Sam set the chair back on all four legs and sat down.

Officer Burns asked her if she had met George prior to the

cruise."

She shook her head. "No, all of them are new acquaintances this week."

Officer Seger asked George similar questions to those posed to Sam. Had he met her or their other dinner companions prior to the cruise?

At Sam and George's denials, the two officers nodded at each other and pulled two tables together. Officer Burns waved a hand, signalling Sam and George to sit across the table from the two officers.

"Okay, what is all this about?" asked George. "I am beyond curious."

"Kathleen Zackery is missing." Sam shared.

George's jaw dropped. "You are kidding me!"

"Unfortunately, this is no kidding matter, Mr. Simpson," responded Officer Burns. "And we need your assistance."

"Not only are you a table mate with the missing woman," added Officer Seger, "we appreciate that you might have some insight due to your previous career."

George turned to Sam and whispered. "Retired cop. Regina Police Service. And yes, I know who you are and no I am not outing you. I don't think you should either. It would only complicate things."

Sam nodded and then swallowed. *What was the saying?* she thought. *Wherever you go, there you are. Your past is never past you.*

Regina was over 200 kilometers from Saskatoon, where the kidnapping occurred. If George were on the force six years ago then he would certainly know who she was.

Face it, she chided herself. *Everyone in western Canada knows who you are and your part in your nephew's death.*

She wondered if George saw her as a victim or a participant. Her light-hearted pal George had turned into an accuser before her eyes.

"Ms. Anderson, can you tell me about your day yesterday, when you were with the sisters and what you saw and heard?" asked Officer Burns.

Sam was pulled out of the past and into the present with the officer's question. She pulled out her notebook for reference.

At the officer's glance at her notebook, she mumbled, "I jotted a few notes down as soon as I heard she was missing. Once a journalist, as they say...." She flipped over to the first page of her notes.

"I first saw the two sisters ahead of me in the line-up to get off the ship. I didn't know at that time that I would be on the same excursion to the glacier or that we would spend time together."

"How did you know it was them?"

"They were wearing matching Alaska jackets, one in ivory with a blue lining and one in navy with an ivory lining. They were hatless, and although their hair is the same blonde, Kathleen had hers in a twist and Lauren had hers loose around her shoulders."

"You didn't plan to leave the ship together?"

"No, we met up on the bus for the excursion to the Mendenhall Glacier and from there Lauren and I went to see the old Orthodox Church in downtown Juneau and Kathleen took a taxi to the Glacier Gardens."

"Did Mrs. Zackery tell you if she had any other plans or was going to meet anyone?" asked Burns.

"No, in fact there was just a general understanding that she would be going back to the ship after the Gardens and Lauren and I would be going back to the ship after seeing the church."

"Is that what happened?"

"No, after we returned to the waterfront, we stopped for a drink and then we separated.

"That was at the Twisted Fish?" Burns asked.

"Yes," she smiled."

"Something you wish to add?"

"Lauren had a friendly conversation with the barman over the contrasting merits of Guinness and the Stout from Alaskan Brewing."

"She flirted?"

"She is married, not dead, officer. And he was rather handsome."

Burns harrumphed and continued with his questions. "After you left the restaurant, did you continue together to the ship?"

"No, there were a couple of shops I wished to have a glance through. I said that I didn't expect her to stay with me and shop and she said that she would see me at dinner."

"So you didn't board with Mrs. Williams?"

"No, but George may have run into her or Kathleen on the gangway." She nodded towards George who had given her a 'why did you drag me into this' look?

"Mr. Simpson?"

"I left the ship late in the day as I had fallen and had to be taken to the medical clinic aboard."

The officers grimaced in sympathy, glancing at George's sling.

"And..." Officer Seger prompted.

"I ran into, well I observed, one of the two sisters, not sure which one, I hate to say, I was not very observant at the moment as I was trying to get off the ship for an hour or so before..."

"And she was..." the same officer prompted.

"Organizing herself. That is the only way I can describe it. She had her jacket twisted around and her scarf was on the floor. I don't know if someone had run into her. She didn't seem upset, only disorganized."

"Now Ms. Anderson and Mr. Simpson," asked the Officer Burns, "do you think that Mr. Zackery, Mrs. Williams or Mr. Williams are capable of doing harm to Mrs. Zackery?"

After a moment of reflection, Sam remarked, "Lauren and Rupert seem to genuinely love and care for each other. They are quite demonstrative in their affection for each other. Daniel and Kathleen, however, seem tense and awkward in each other's company. Beyond that, I can't say."

George nodded, "That is a fair assessment of their relationships. Whether any one of them would cause Kathleen harm is a different kettle of fish."

"Is there anything else that you think may be pertinent?" Officer Burns asked.

Sam decided to keep silent about the strange conversation that Daniel was having over the phone in the gangway. That would drag her photographic assistant James into this mess and Daniel's words could have been irrelevant.

"Quite a mystery, eh?" George said, shaking his head. "Any idea?"

"None," replied Officer Burns, placing the lid on his pen and placing it purposefully on top of the legal pad. "First, people die on ships every day, but usually due to ill health not foul play. Second, if Mrs. Zackery had gone overboard in daylight, chances are someone would have seen her. The Juneau docks are busy and people are always gazing at and photographing the large cruise ships. Thanks to the latitude and time of year, we had good light quite late, even up till 10 p.m. when Mr. Zackery made us aware of his wife's absence. Third, the two sisters were scanned in within fifteen minutes of each other, and our computers report Mrs. Zackery to be on board, yet no staff member can confirm with certainty that she did actually come aboard."

"Fourth," Officer Seger added, "We have searched the entire ship excluding the passenger cabins, which will be searched as soon as the stewards have a valid reason to access, such as morning straightening. We have found nothing."

Officer Burns sat back in his chair, "I really am hoping that she had a fight with the husband, tied one on, took a stranger to bed and we will find her hungover in a stranger's cabin later this morning."

"That seems highly unlikely from what I have seen of her character," George suggested, ruefully. "But, I too hope for a quick and safe resolution to this situation."

"What is next? The police? We are still in American waters, but the ship is not registered in the United States and the Zackerys are Canadians," asked Sam.

"We will be reporting back to the Captain immediately and then he will decide what action will be taken," Officer Burns said, closing up the computer with the security records. "We want to keep this as close to the chest as possible until we know more. We don't want any kind of panic or any amateur detectives scouring the ship. Once we have done a cabin-by-cabin search and if she is still missing, we will figure out the jurisdictional issues. If she is not on the boat, then it may be Juneau or Canada's case."

"Without someone having seen her fall or jump overboard, the authorities won't know where to search," George mused, "The ocean is a big place. If she was pushed...."

"Foul play is possible," said Officer Burns rubbing his chin with its day and a half's growth. "But I hate to even think about murder.

"Kidnapping is very rare in these situations, too. But we are quite clueless as to what could have occurred," he summarized, shaking his head. The two officers stood, pushed their chairs into the table and left.

"Kidnapping isn't as rare as you may think." Sam said to their retreating backs.

CHAPTER TWENTY-TWO

Sam and George looked around the well-lit, empty and gaudy room. "Quite something isn't it?" Sam commented.

She turned to George and noticed the disappearance of the white tape that had adorned his glasses the evening before. "You fixed your glasses?" she asked.

George smiled, "In a way. At least we have one mystery solved. I have walked into walls, missed steps, missed docks, and generally have been off kilter since I boarded this ship. The day before I left Regina, I had picked up my new glasses. I left my old ones at home as I was glad to have my new pair as they are progressive lenses and would help with reading small print. Apparently, the optical shop confused my new glasses with ones for another George Simpson. I really do have a twin out there after all," he laughed. "Well, at least the same name and same glasses frames!

"He got my new glasses and I got his. He finally brought his back to the optical shop to complain. He was tripping over things as well. They solved the mystery and called me to ask me to come in for an exchange, but I had already left for the cruise and I haven't checked messages since I left. My daughter went to my house to check on things and listened to my voice mail. She picked up my new glasses and sent them by Federal Express to Skagway. This morning they were at the purser's office. Apparently, I am not becoming a klutz after all."

"Oh, George." Sam and George laughed and then sobered up as awareness of the situation returned.

"What a sorry mess this is," he said.

"My thoughts exactly," Sam agreed. They sat for another few moments, deep in their own thoughts.

"So," he asked, clearing his throat. "Do you mind me asking? You don't seem to be living high off the hog. What did you do with the money?"

"What do you know so far?"

"After you won the lottery, your nephew was kidnapped and before you could pay the ransom, he died."

"That is true. All of it. I spent some of it initially paying off my debts and house mortgage and the debts and mortgages of my sister and my brother. I realized about that point that I had spent enough. In the end, you can only spend so much, buy so much, shop so much.

"Don't get me wrong, I wasn't like one of those lottery winners who don't think they are worthy or feel guilty about winning millions of dollars. But underneath it all, when I looked at what my life was becoming and the people I was attracting, I knew that I needed to resolve my relationship with the lottery money. The money, which should have been a golden gift, was itself becoming a burden. I wanted to do something useful and good in the world with this unexpected windfall.

"I had just started the process of creating a private foundation when my nephew, Tristan, was kidnapped. After his death. I was glad I had decided to give it away. No one wanted anything to do with the money. Not my brother, not my sister and not me. I began the foundation and donated the $53 million."

"All of it!" George exclaimed.

"Yes, all of it. Well, most of it. I put one million into a locked in GIC account for myself, and one for my brother and one for my sister. Who knows what the price of elder care will be by the time we are in our eighties?"

George laughed, "You don't think you will regret donating the money to the foundation? Can you ever access it?"

"No, it's gone. A board of governors manages all of the operations. I just bring projects to their attention that I think can be helped."

"So the travel writing is a ruse?"

"No, I really do write travel articles for OOTA. They really do pay me. Just not much. The magazine is not in the ranks of Condé Nast Traveler, but it is a publication that I am proud of writing for and that I believe brings value to the reader.

"The fund managers for the foundation also manage the $450,000 I sold the house for and," she smiled, "they are very, very good. With that additional income, I write what I want to write, and travel the world investigating possible projects for the foundation."

"What kind of projects does this foundation of yours fund?"

"Anything which helps those who have had a bad shot at life. Bursaries for single mothers, schools in Central America, and lately some water wells in Africa. It's my way of balancing the social disadvantage some people were born with or acquired."

"That is why the Corey Art Project interested you?"

"Both to fund, but also to perhaps write about."

"It doesn't sound like a travel article."

"I also write for the on-line magazine, Global Perspective. They sometimes take articles from me that balance social justice."

"I've heard of that publication. Aren't they kind of whistle blowers against white collar criminals?"

"Partly. They also cover financial news, especially scams."

"Isn't its editor a renegade, sort of like Julian Assange?"

Sam laughed, "I don't know about that. I have never met him. I haven't even spoken to him. We correspond totally through email. Editorially, though, he definitely is on the edge. Not on the edge of outing global military secrets like WikiLeaks, grant you, but definitely he has a following."

"What would you be doing now if you hadn't won the money?"

"After finishing my degree in Journalism, I realized that a very select few of us would ever write full-time for a daily newspaper or anchor a nightly news show. It is just the nature of the profession. As my heart is really in photojournalism and the written word, feature writing allowed me to write the sort of articles I enjoyed investigating and left room for other better paying work."

"Such as...?"

"Now don't laugh. It isn't glamorous or exciting."

"What?"

"Technical sales documents."

"So the technical writing field has lost your fine work but the charitable world has gained an advocate."

"That is a complimentary assessment. Do you miss the excitement of policing?"

"People often think police work is exciting. In a way it is. But generally it is long stretches of boredom interspersed with short bursts of high stress and adrenaline. And those short bursts were usually followed by long hours of paperwork. After 25 years I was happy to be done and out. I keep my hand in the mix, working with a couple of private investigators now and then."

"Well I think I have a story to investigate and you have a mystery to solve."

George leaned over the table and they shook hands on their new partnership.

CHAPTER TWENTY-THREE

Daniel was in the ship's pub, The Rover, sitting at the bar, his third whisky down. The pub had opened only half an hour before and he was the only customer. He played with the paper coaster as he deliberated his strategy, turning the coaster on its edges like a square wheel.

How should he approach Lauren about his handling the trust investments? Now would be the best time while she seemed in shock. Would it be better to have Rupert ask her? Fifteen days left.

Lauren sat in the Champagne Bar across the way. Her second mimosa was still not taking the edge off the almost lies she had told. *How much of this would come back to haunt her? Or send her to jail?* How she missed Kathleen already.

Rupert paced the hall in his cabin. Eight feet one direction, turn, eight feet back. The steward knocked on the door before entering to straighten the cabin. One glance at Rupert's scowl, he dropped his grin and began to back out of the room, apologizing for the interruption. Rupert continued his pacing. *Could Lauren really believe that he would harm her? Or harm Kathleen?* His life was falling apart.

CHAPTER TWENTY-FOUR

Sam perused the menu, sitting alone at the table for six. She had spent the day touring the Aboriginal art of Ketchikan. The area was still a strong centre for the Tlingit and Haida peoples and the Totem Bight State Historical Park helped to preserve their native Alaskan history and art. Sam had gazed at the sky-reaching totems and learned the story behind each element on the fourteen poles. She thought how interested both Kathleen and Lauren would have been in bringing this art form and its significance to the Corey Art Project.

As a Canadian, Sam was well aware of the totem pole. They were common in British Columbia, but seeing so many historical totems, all constructed with products from nature, in one place. It just gave her goose bumps.

Sam had declined the remainder of the excursion, which included the Ketchikan city tour and the lumberjack show, choosing to remain at the centre and learn more.

She looked at the menu again. Did she walk enough today to balance the decadent choices? *Enough to balance the Roast Gressingham Duck with Apple and Cranberry Savoury Stuffing? Or should I stick with the grilled fish?*

Talking about the lottery win with George had been unsettling. At 32 years of age, she could see many years of travelling, writing, and project discovery before her. Travelling the world and investigating projects was fulfilling work. She knew that many people were positively affected by the different projects the foundation sponsored.

She was content that her writing made a difference for the armchair travellers who couldn't or wouldn't leave the safety or comfort of their own homes but escaped their daily lives through the travel adventures she lived and documented. She also knew from her fan mail that she had inspired readers to shake off the familiar and to step into an adventure that she had already confirmed as safe and achievable.

Yet, for a moment, George had reminded her about the world she had surrendered. First class seats on airplanes, suites on cruise ships, designer clothes. The images flew past and were replaced by the wonder of a woman able to pump safe water from a well in her village instead of walking a mile each morning to an unclean source.

The waiter appeared at her elbow and quietly let her know that none of her fellow tablemates would be joining her this evening. Would she like to move to another table where there was an opening or eat alone?

Where is George? She wondered.

Day Six

Aboard the ship Sea Wanderer and sailing the Inside Passage

Grilled Lamb Cutlets, Roasted Vegetables and Bell Pepper Coulis

Or

Lobster Thermidor with Truffle Scented Pilaf Rice

Or

Beef Wellington, Dauphine Potatoes and Madeira Truffle Sauce

CHAPTER TWENTY-FIVE

"Rappelling dates back to 1876 when Jean Charlet-Straton from France perfected the controlled descent down a rock face using a rope," Sam wrote. "Generally used when a cliff is too steep or dangerous to descend without support, rappelling is also an exhilarating out of the ordinary travel adventure."

"Rock climbing is not for the faint of heart, but neither is it out of reach for the reasonably fit adventurer," Sam typed.

Finishing the article, Sam sent a quick email with the draft article to her fact checker, John, to verify the definitions and history and a second email to her editor at OOTA. Then, she logged off.

Stretching to relieve her back and neck muscles, she walked around her cabin and wondered if she and George would be at the table alone tonight. Had the mysterious Kathleen been found? If not, would the other three be there for dinner?

A knock on her cabin door stirred her out her wonderings

and she checked her image in the mirror on the closet before answering. She has a habit of running her fingers through her short, red hair when writing, giving her an Albert Einstein mad scientist hairdo.

Seeing George through the peephole, she ushered him in quickly. "I was sorry to have missed you last night at dinner," she said.

"I wanted to do a little research before we left good internet and cell service in Ketchikan. You may be surprised to hear what I learned. Ahh, the beauty of the web."

George sat on the only chair in the room and Sam sat on the corner of the bed.

"Although I spent my years on the police force in Saskatchewan, I have plenty of contacts in Vancouver. I wanted to find out what I could about the three players in this mystery."

"What did you find out?"

"Our friend Daniel is broke. He owned a condo in West Vancouver overlooking Howe Sound – apparently that is one of the most upscale areas to live on the lower mainland."

"Owned?"

"Technically, it is in his name, but he mortgaged it to the hilt a month ago."

"Would Kathleen have known?"

"It is only in his name. I assume he bought it before their marriage."

"What else?"

"All of his lines of credit are maxed out, even his business ones."

"What about the equity in his brokerage firm?"

"He doesn't owe salaries to anyone but he has payables in 60 and 90 day columns. However, the big negative is that his firm is on its way down the toilet. He focuses on high worth clients and they are leaving him in droves and the ones that are staying are keeping their assets in money markets."

"Which don't create good commissions," Sam mused. "So there is a confidence issue?"

"He has a reputation of playing high roller stakes, investing in high risk, high reward stocks and other 'instruments' as my buddy calls them."

"What about his own portfolio. Surely he has secure investments himself?" asked Sam.

"Nope. Not that I can find. He invests in penny stock junior resource companies that are being aggressively promoted. Once the share prices rise 10 or so cents, he dumps them. He plays with other investors who do the same thing. It is called pump and dump."

"So they leave other investors holding the bag when they get out and the stock price drops," Sam said, shaking her head.

"Occasionally Zachery even steered some of his own clients into investing in the same companies that he was at the moment himself dumping."

"But with the economic markets, aren't investors becoming less risk tolerant?" Sam asked.

"He's losing clients and soon his house of cards will crumble," George said.

"But is that enough for him to kill his wife?" Sam asked.

CHAPTER TWENTY-SIX

Daniel printed off the *Request for Insurance Equity Loan* document in the internet café on the Sea Wanderer.

With Kathleen's life insurance policy beside him, he completed the form, forging her signature and pre-dating the request to the day before the cruise departed Vancouver. The form requested half of the cash value of the policy, $500,000, in an equity loan.

If her body was found, and she was declared dead, the advance loan would be deducted off the amount of the five million life insurance payment that he would receive as her beneficiary.

Daniel typed a cover sheet for the fax. To the insurance company and their fax number, from K. B. Zackery and the fax number at the office at Corey Art Project.

He walked to the back of the internet café and slowly faxed the cover sheet and two page request form. He had asked for the cheque to be mailed to their condo address. The cheque would be in Kathleen's name and he would deposit it into their joint account. He would then write a cheque to the 'boys.' It wasn't the original plan, but he only had fourteen days left.

CHAPTER TWENTY-SEVEN

"When you're travelling, you don't have to actually stop moving to take a good picture," Sam began her lecture entitled *Photography on the Go*.

Let's discuss the techniques professional photographers use to take a shot on the run," Sam stood at the front of the card room and smiled at her class of thirty-two avid, amateur photographers.

She was surprised to see Lauren in the class. *No doubt taking an opportunity to distract herself until tomorrow morning when we dock in Vancouver*, Sam thought. It was only 48 hours ago that Lauren, Kathleen and she had been trekking around the Mendenhall Glacier. So much had happened since. Before the workshop had begun, Sam had asked Lauren quietly if there was any news. The other woman had just shaken her head wordlessly, turned and sat down at a nearby table.

"Let's talk about taking pictures from an airplane. This is when seat selection really matters. First, try to get a window seat.

Secondly, when choosing the left or right side of the plane, take into consideration what sites will be visible out each side and more importantly from which direction will the sun be shining during flight. Choose the side away from the sun to avoid shooting into the glare."

The rest of the hour flew by as the avid photographers asked their questions about taking photos on the go. They filed out chatting with each other and enthusiastically clicking through images on their cameras. Soon only George was in the room with her. He had come in half-way through the presentation and was sitting quietly in the back.

"I wanted to catch you and this is the only place I knew you definitely would be before dinner."

"Would you like to go somewhere for a coffee?"

"Let's talk here. I don't want to be overheard." George closed the door.

Sam left her equipment on the front table and took the chair beside George.

"Did you find out something more?"

"Rupert is pretty much what you see, except he likes to gamble. In fact, I sat in on a game with him earlier today. I wanted to gauge his desperation. Did he seem to react as if he owned money to anyone, that kind of thing."

"And?"

"Not that I can see. I did casually ask him about his career in banking, making a little joke about gambling being perhaps a better way to increase my assets considering the low interest rates banks and credit unions are providing these days.

"One of the other fellows at the table mentioned that the banks are under a lot of financial pressure as well, what with the low interest rates, sluggish economy and all. The same fellow mentioned that Rupert's bank was going through a merger. Rupert just mumbled at that. If his organization is going through a change, he might be nervous about that affecting his job security and prospects."

"But if he was involved in Kathleen's disappearance, what does he gain?" Sam asked.

"If she is declared dead, Daniel gets the life insurance and Lauren gets 100% control over the millions. I suppose being married to Lauren would then change things, but only if he convinced her to divert some of the money to them to use personally, not to just invest for the good of the charity."

"What about Lauren?" asked Sam. "Did you find out anything there?"

"The couple live in Kerrisdale."

"I know where that is. It's an affluent neighbourhood on Vancouver's west side and is a mix of newer and older homes and low-rise condos and apartments. Quite a mix of professionals, students in basement apartments and the very wealthy in the newer monster homes, often built by newcomers from Hong Kong."

"They live in a fairly large two story house. The Corey Art Project's offices are on the main floor and Lauren and Rupert have a separate apartment on the top floor. The Corey Art Project rents the lower space. Lauren's parents lived there with the girls when they were growing up. The house is now owned jointly by Lauren and Kathleen, but if Kathleen dies it goes directly to Lauren not to Daniel."

"Poor Rupert – doesn't even get to own his own home," Sam tsked. "I wonder how he feels about that."

"One more asset to go to Lauren if Kathleen is dead."

"Enough motivation to go around."

"You've said it," agreed George.

CHAPTER TWENTY-EIGHT

Lobster Thermidor with Truffle Scented Pilaf Rice or Beef Wellington, Dauphine Potatoes and Madeira Truffle Sauce.

"Most people put weight on when they take a cruise," Sam said to George. Her auburn red hair slid forward as she lowered her head to read the menu. She wore a navy and white striped sundress with a white wool shawl over her shoulders.

They were the first two at the table for six.

"Doesn't look to me like you put weight on this week," said George, admiringly. If he was twenty years younger, he would attempt a more romantic relationship. But she seemed to be a rolling stone that gathered no moss and he was a divorced old guy with a house in Regina, a boat at the Regina Beach marina and four grandkids.

"Thanks George," Sam smiled, patting him on the sleeve. "You are good for my ego. The rappelling, climbing and walking this week helped, but I still had to work out twice." She looked down at her menu. "Everything sounds so wonderful," she said.

"Worse. Everything tastes so wonderful!"

Sam laughed.

"I wonder if we will see the others, this being our last dinner at sea," George mused aloud.

"I was surprised to see Lauren in my workshop today. When she left she said she would see me later, but..." Sam looked up in time to see Daniel, Lauren and Rupert approach the table.

"Well, here you are," she said encouragingly as they sat down. "George and I were wondering if we would see you tonight."

As they sat, and before Sam could ask the latest development on Kathleen's disappearance, Lauren asked, "Are those new glasses, George?"

As George retold the tale of his spectacle mix-up, Sam watched the others.

Lauren smiled at George's tale, but there were stress lines around her mouth where she held her smile tightly. Daniel and Rupert both looked like they hadn't slept. Their clothing was neat enough, but their rounded postures gave away their tired disposition.

"I suppose you are curious as to what the officers have found?" asked Rupert.

"Not a damn thing is what!" Daniel exploded. "Apparently we can't even declare her missing until who knows when!"

Lauren added calmly, "The RCMP have taken a missing person's report. The ship security officers have done a thorough search of the ship. All private, public and crew areas have been searched. They have found nothing.

"They can't make up their minds as to what likely happened.

Did she get back on the ship in Juneau? Did she disembark again before the ship left port? They have no idea," Daniel informed them all. "I can't just bide my time until this is resolved. This issue needs to be resolved immediately!"

Sam and George looked at each other. *His wife's life or death is merely an issue to be resolved?*

"Well, we are pleased you could join us for dinner," Sam said, speaking for herself and George.

Daniel took the menu from the waiter who had approached their table. "Well there is nothing else to do until we dock in Vancouver."

"Any news at all?" Sam asked Lauren.

"No, nothing."

The stress of the situation was certainly wearing on Lauren, Sam thought. The blonde had dark half circles beneath her eyes.

"I suppose you will be glad to get back to Vancouver," Sam said quietly to Lauren. "It must be difficult to get any satisfaction with the authorities when they aren't sure what happened."

"Idiots," Daniel muttered through clenched teeth. "Alaskan police could do nothing. As far as the RCMP is concerned it is not their jurisdiction, but as Lauren said, they did do a missing person's report. The damn ship is registered in Panama so apparently follows laws according to that jurisdiction. So who the hell knows what that might mean. The security people on board ship have no idea what to do. The Alaskan police believe that Kathleen re-boarded in Juneau. The ship security systems show that she was scanned in when she came back on board but no one really saw her from that point on. So the ship security is challenging that she even came back on board."

"Idiot cops." Daniel looked into his glass of wine and mentally wandered off.

I looked at George. He shrugged. Neither of us were about to tell Daniel that George was an idiot cop. His past career had not come up in conversation to this point so better to leave sleeping dogs lie.

"I am glad that you are getting away from all this when we get home," Rupert said to Lauren, patting her hand. "I just wish you would let me join you."

Lauren looked up to Sam's questioning look. "My parents always took a trip the week of their wedding anniversary. Since they died, Kathleen and I have been retracing their steps in a way by revisiting the locations, sometimes even the same hotels, where they stayed. This year more than anything, I need to feel them around me. Spiritually speaking, that is. I am going ahead with the plans that Kathleen and I made over a year ago."

"What?" Daniel asked, pulling himself to the present. "Where are you going? Where are you staying? Is Rupert going with you?"

"I am going by myself, Daniel. I don't want to pull Rupert away from work and I want some alone time in New Orleans just to think. Don't worry, I will be fine."

Day Seven

Disembarking the ship Sea Wanderer and Vancouver

Fanny Bay Oysters served on Braised Kale with Béchamel Sauce and Bourbon Bacon Jam

Or

Fried Green Tomato with Panko-Crusted Grilled Black Tiger Prawns and Shrimp Remoulade

Or

Louisiana Blue Crab Cakes with Fire-roasted Red Pepper Remoulade

CHAPTER TWENTY-NINE

Chewies on West Hastings specialized in New Orleans cooking and it quickly was becoming one of Sam's favourite Vancouver spots. It also had been a quick walk from the cruise ship terminal, even with her rolling suitcase and laptop/camera bag in tow.

She perused the menu while her mind continued to drift back to the missing Kathleen. No disappearance of a person is normal; however, all the missing pieces in Kathleen's situation drove her curiosity to the point where she found it difficult to think of anything else but the mystery.

If Kathleen had run away from her life, how did she get off the ship? If she was on the ship, why couldn't they find her or her body? Nothing was missing from her room except the clothes she had worn ashore to Juneau.

Even Lauren's passport and room key were in her room. *If she left the cabin willingly, wouldn't she have taken her room key? If she had planned to leave Alaska, she would have surely needed her passport to re-enter Canada,* Sam's thoughts whirled, settling back to the same unanswered questions.

Her wallet with her credit cards was found in the safe. Had she gone overboard? Was something even further sinister afoot?

Sam's attention returned to the menu before her. *Grilled black tiger prawns, parmesan-panko crusted tomatoes, bacon, and shrimp remoulade.* Smiling, Sam ordered the *Fried Green Tomato and Prawn* appetizer and then sat back to people watch the late Vancouver lunch crowd.

Her phone rang. Pulling it from her bag, she smiled at her OOTA editor's number. "Hello, Blackie! How are you?"

"I can hardly hear you," yelled her editor. "Where the hell are you? No, don't tell me, you are at a restaurant. Didn't you get enough on the cruise ship?"

"You know I wouldn't have eaten since early this morning." There was no love lost by Sam for the long disembarking process at the end of a cruise. "All that queuing up makes a girl hungry." She nodded and smiled to the server as the green tomato dish was set in front of her.

"I love the two articles you have sent me. We can use the Mendenhall Glacier article in a couple of months. I may have a spa tour set up for you starting in 45 days."

"Wait! Wait! Spa tour? As in Discovery Shores Boracay in the Philippines. The Four Seasons Hotel Spa in Chiang Mai, Thailand. Canyon Ranch in..."

"Do we need to have the 'We are not Condé Nast!' conversation?" interrupted her editor. "We are dependent on advertising revenue and focus on sponsored adventures or..."

"I know, I know, close to home locations," Sam finished her

editor's sentence.

Condé Nast Traveler is a premier travel magazine. In each issue, it stated that they do not accept free or discounted trips and accommodation in exchange for editorial coverage. Their editors and reporters pay the same prices their readers pay and travel unannounced, except in rare cases where it is impossible to do so. This ensures, the magazine states, that their editors and writers travel the way their readers do, with no special recognition, treatment or obligation and are therefore free to report their findings honestly with no conflict of interest or ulterior motive. They are the truth in travel.

Condé Nast's policy of publishing articles not related to advertisers and paying fully for the privilege of doing so was an ongoing joke between Sam and her editor. OOTA was a small scale magazine focused on encouraging people to venture out of their travel comfort zones. If they couldn't travel far, then OOTA's second goal was to publish such friendly and compelling pieces that their readers lived vicariously through the adventures of the magazine's writers. Condé Nast only published pieces where the travel writers had not been paid in any way by the location covered. This was certainly a noble philosophy, Blackie agreed, but not a realistic one for her five-year-old publication.

Sam was anxious to get to her appetizer, but she needed to know. "How local?"

"Local to you at the moment. The first one for you to visit would be the Willow Stream Spa at The Fairmont Banff Springs."

Sam thought about the historic hotel nestled in the magnificent Canadian Rockies. "What a fabulous hotel. I remember it as a combination of a French Chateau, a Swiss chalet and a Scottish castle."

"I can't say I have been there," said her editor, calling from New Mexico. Sam could hear Blackie flipping through her notes. "Built in 1888, it sounds fantastic."

"I look forward to hearing the full plan. In the meantime, I have decided to work on a music and food article. I will send it to you as soon as I am finished and you can have first nod. If it isn't a fit, I have a couple other magazines that might want it."

"Let me see it first," her editor barked. "Where are you going?"

"New Orleans."

CHAPTER THIRTY

"I think it would be a good idea if you stayed another day or so here in Vancouver," Rupert suggested, watching Lauren pack.

As she pulled out the warmer wear she had needed for Alaska and replaced them with the sundresses and sandals she would need for the Big Easy, she shook her head.

"Rupert, my flight is already booked." Lauren had a 2:20 p.m. Air Canada flight to New Orleans through Denver arriving at 11:04 p.m. central standard time.

"I am worried about how you are handling this... this...," her husband floundered, not certain how to term the disappearance and probable death of his wife's twin sister.

Lauren put down the blouse in her hand and placed her hands on Rupert's cheeks and kissed him softly. "I'm not going to reschedule it. I'm going tomorrow."

Rupert pulled her in for a tight hug. She spoke, her voice

muffled against his neck. "I can't do anything here. Maybe I'll feel closer to Kathleen there."

And maybe I will feel less guilty with the lies I have told you, she thought.

CHAPTER THIRTY-ONE

Joe Fortes Seafood and Chop House in downtown Vancouver was buzzing with excitement with the usual 5 p.m. after-work crowd.

Daniel was stewing. As he savoured the crispness of the Spirit Bear Gin in his martini, he thought *what a mess*.

If Kathleen's body was found he could push for a quick life insurance settlement. Without it being found, he needed to make sure the disappearance was not made public until he received the loan against the equity of her life insurance policy.

Only the fact that the cruise ship wanted to mitigate any negative publicity regarding Kathleen's disappearance from their ship prevented the incident from being picked up by the media, he thought. Yet without media pressure and a belief in their jurisdiction involvement, the police and cruise line were unlikely to take action towards finding the body. Except for questioning him and those Kathleen knew on the ship, the security team aboard had done little. He was left in limbo.

He couldn't call the life insurance company to ask how long he had to wait before Kathleen could be declared dead and he could secure the full life insurance benefit. That would trigger closer scrutiny of the loan. *As would media attention, damn it.*

Back to plan A. Lauren was taking off today for New Orleans for her week away and seemed strangely determined to go in spite of the situation. He had pressed Rupert to ask Lauren about the paperwork for the millions before she left and Rupert had said that she would find it a strange request coming so quickly on the heels of Kathleen's disappearance. Give him a couple of days, Rupert had requested of Daniel, and he would ask her again.

Daniel spun the remaining liquid in his martini glass around and around, hoping for a magical answer in the vermouth and gin.

"Would you like to order any food, Mr. Zackery?" the barman asked his regular customer. Joe Fortes restaurant was an award winning Vancouver restaurant and one of Daniels's favourite haunts. He often came to the restaurant on Thurlow Street after work or with clients to take advantage of the oyster bar. The food was exceptional and it was nice to go where they remembered your name. It was his 'Cheers.'

The restaurant was named after Joe Fortes, a Vancouver legend who was a local character who had taught hundreds of children to swim, saving many lives. He was immortalized with a monument in Stanley Park, with the tag 'Little Children Loved Him.' Somehow Daniel felt like he had a kinship with Joe. They both had a 'take charge' kind of attitude.

"No, I'm good."

The words were no quicker out of his mouth, when two

gentlemen took the bar stools to the left and right of his. He recognized them as fellow investors in the latest pump and dump. The bartender looked at them to see if they wanted service, but they were focused on Daniel.

"Funny meeting you here, Daniel," said the man to his left.

"Feel like buying us a drink?" said the other.

Under other circumstances he would have welcomed their company. Now as he nodded to the bar man to bring a round, he was reminded that there may be no more drinks at Joe Fortes in the future. No more 'someone knowing his name.' Thirteen days left.

Day Eight

Vancouver and New Orleans

Mango Crab Nigiri

Or

Crispy California Roll

Or

Lobster Roll

CHAPTER THIRTY-TWO

Sam parked on West 41st Avenue and walked the two blocks to the office of the Corey Art Project where she easily weaseled Lauren's cell number and hotel location from Lauren's assistant, Carole. Luckily, Lauren had already spoken to her assistant about Sam's possible article featuring the Corey Art Project so Carole was more than amiable about sharing Lauren's personal information.

Walking down to West 41st Avenue, Sam passed her parked rental car and continued west to the Kerrisdale shopping district. On the south side of the street across and down one block from the ubiquitous Starbucks, she entered Irashai, the sushi restaurant recommended by Lauren's assistant. She ordered the house red wine and the lobster roll and settled in for an hour of gastronomical bliss.

She had just missed Lauren who had taken a taxi to the nearby Skytrain stop at the Oakridge Mall. From there it would be a mere ten minutes to the Vancouver airport and Lauren's flight to New Orleans. Sam would be taking the same train to the airport the next morning, but from the Waterfront station farther downtown.

Sam took out her notepad and continued her notes regarding the perplexing missing twin mystery, as she had decided to term it.

CHAPTER THIRTY-THREE

Lauren walked through the security scanner at the Vancouver International airport and smiled at the security agent. She pulled her shoes from the plastic bin and put them on with one hand, gathering her bag and scarf with the other. Already she could feel the release of tension that had gripped her since the day she disembarked the Sea Wanderer in Juneau. She couldn't even risk letting Rupert drive her to the airport, she was concerned that she would break down and tell him everything.

CHAPTER THIRTY-FOUR

"Bollocks!" Rupert exclaimed. *Why hadn't she let him take her to the airport?*

He knew he had to be cautious about taking time off work for personal business during this time of transition and layoffs, but these were extraordinary circumstances.

There must be something more we can do! He thought. Lauren had asked him not to mention Kathleen's disappearance as she wanted to keep it from the media as long as possible with the hope that they would know more before it became public. She wanted to avoid the inevitable media frenzy as long as possible. He somewhat disagreed with her point of view, but he was taking her lead on all things regarding Kathleen. Lauren was Kathleen's sister; after all, he was only a brother in law.

When his landline rang, he picked it up quickly after reading the number identified.

"Have you heard anything, Daniel?" he asked.

"No, did you ask her?"

"No, I ..." Rupert explained, but the line was already dead.

"Bloody asshole," He said under his breath.

Day Nine

Vancouver and New Orleans

Balsamic Braised Beef Short Ribs
slow braised to fork tender, mashed potatoes, asparagus

Or

Lobster and Florentine Ravioli
Artisan-made Spinach & Artichoke filled ravioli,
crispy prosciutto, tomato caper tapenade

Or

Bombay Butter Chicken
with Aromatic Almond Basmati Rice and Grilled
Naan bread

CHAPTER THIRTY-FIVE

It was only 10 a.m. and another New Orleans sweltering day was in the making.

Lauren glanced nervously at her watch as she stood in line at the Federal Express counter in the Marriott hotel on Canal Street. The air conditioning in the hotel was a cool change from the overwhelming heat and humidity outside.

The breeze and cooler outside temperature that had greeted her when she had arrived in New Orleans last night at midnight were gone. The mid-morning heat and humidity of the crescent city hit her like a hot, wet blanket the moment she had left the air conditioning of the Hotel Monteleone. The four-block stroll to the Fed Ex office felt like walking through a steam bath.

She put the passport into an envelope, the envelope into a FedEx envelope, addressed it, gave it to the counter agent, paid with cash and walked away. Guaranteed to arrive by ten a.m. the next morning at its location. *You had to love FedEx*, she thought with a smile.

She had arrived last night and had settled comfortably into the double room she had booked months ago for her and Kathleen to celebrate their parents' marriage and lives. As with every trip with her sister since they were old enough to share a hotel room by themselves, Lauren had taken the bed closest to the bath, the left set of bureau drawers and left side of the wardrobe.

The city beckoned. She had nothing but time on her hands. A walk down Royal Street in the French Quarter? The street held the best antique shops in the city, most likely the best French antiques in North America, and was the original shopping street in the days prior to the Louisiana Purchase.

Lauren turned off Canal to walk the few blocks down Decatur to Jackson Square with its impressive St. Louis Cathedral, Cabildo and 20,000 pound statue of Andrew Jackson on a horse with its granite base inscription 'The Union Must and Shall be Preserved.'

The St. Louis Cathedral was the third structure built on the site, the first being built by the Canadian, Jean-Baptiste Le Moyne who founded New Orleans on behalf of the French. To the left of the Cathedral was the Cabildo. Built in the late 1700s, it served as the seat of government before France sold the terrain to the Americans. Lauren felt as a Canadian, she should at least spend a moment in the square to honour Le Moyne.

Two blocks further down Decatur, she stopped at the Café du Monde. The temptation of the icing sugar covered beignets and the aroma of chicory coffee by the French market won her inner cultural debate and she asked the maître d' for a table. She joined the people in the outside café, moving slowly in the dense humidity, sighing when a cool breeze off the river occasionally lifted her hair and blew across her face.

CHAPTER THIRTY-SIX

Daniel dialled his cell phone with his right hand while he ran his fingers through his hair with his left. He looked around the condominium that would soon belong solely to the bank if he didn't persevere.

He was feeling like the walls were closing in and although he had promised Rupert time to work on Lauren regarding the reassignment papers, he couldn't wait any longer. He hoped he could convince Lauren to do the right thing while she remained in her current state of denial. He thought the realization of Kathleen's permanent loss had not struck the twin yet and when it did, he may or may not be able to persuade her. She might be even more determined to follow Kathleen's and her parents' ridiculous rules for the investment of the millions once her grieving began.

"Rupert, sorry about hanging up on you earlier. I lost the connection," said Daniel, blaming the cell service company.

"I am thinking about hiring a private detective," he continued, "and I want to speak to Lauren about it. I tried her cell phone but she isn't picking up. Did she fly out today to New Orleans? Which hotel is she at?"

"I don't think she changed the arrangements from before the cruise, Rupert replied.

"The Monteleone then?"

"I think so. Daniel?

"Yes?"

"If she doesn't want to talk about anything, and I mean anything, don't push her. She is very fragile right now."

"No, don't worry, Rupert. I certainly won't," he said hanging up.

He walked to his home office and closed his office door. Somehow that seemed more private, even though he was alone. He connected on line to the Air Canada website and booked his flight.

At his end, Rupert put down the phone. He closed his office door and began to pace. He worried the inside of his mouth, running the tip of his tongue in a circle against the inside of his right cheek, distorting his otherwise pleasant face with the bubble, giving physical evidence of his discomfort.

His usual positive attitude and demeanour had deserted him. He opened the top right hand drawer of his desk and took out the Zantac and Rolaids, and with a cup of cold tea, swallowed two of each.

Day Ten

Vancouver and New Orleans

Cranberry Scones with Devonshire Cream
and Strawberry Jam

French Lemon Tarts

Crustless Cucumber and Smoked Salmon Sandwiches

CHAPTER THIRTY-SEVEN

"I am glad I was able to see you on this trip. Usually you just make a quick stop to change planes in Vancouver and we don't have a chance for a nice long visit," Jillian commented, topping up both of their teacups. It was a blend from Murchie's Teas on West Hastings in Vancouver, one of Sam's favourite tea shops. It was a special ritual that the two women would often share – sipping Murchie's and looking out the window to Jillian's back rose garden.

"And thanks for the accommodation," said Sam, referring to the pull out couch in the study. She stretched her back to make the point that the couch could definitely use a new mattress.

"Hey, beggars can't be choosers," laughed Jill, poking Sam in the arm. The two women had first met in journalism school and had become instant friends. They fell into comfortable conversation each time they saw each other, regardless if it had days or years since their last visit.

Sam took the last French lemon tart off the elegantly arranged afternoon tea tray. Although Jillian was not British, nor originally even from British Columbia, she had been bitten by the elegant afternoon tea ritual. Cranberry Scones with Devonshire Cream and Strawberry Jam, French Lemon Tarts, and Crustless Cucumber and Smoked Salmon Sandwiches were displayed on a layered china plate.

"Who are you staying with in New Orleans or are you at a hotel?" she asked.

"Friends that I met the first year I went to the jazz fest. They live a couple of blocks off St. Charles."

"Isn't St. Charles the avenue the streetcar goes down?"

Jillian had never been to New Orleans. With four teenagers and a full time job as a communications director for a social welfare agency, she had little extra time on her hands to traipse around the world, as she put it. She was one of OOTA's readers who probably would never see the places Sam wrote about but lived vicariously though her travel adventures, seeing the places through the writer's pictures and words.

"One of them. The streetcars run along Canal Street, along the Mississippi River and through the Garden District. My friends live a few blocks off St. Charles in the Garden District so I will be riding back and forth to the French Quarter. Perhaps even on the streetcar named Desire."

"Now, that is just in the play," Jillian chided Sam. "There isn't a real streetcar named Desire."

"Who knows? Some say that the streetcar that inspired Tennessee Williams's play ran in the first Creole neighbourhood of Marigny until 1948, was retired, but might have been brought back into service."

"Those streetcars have been running a long time."

"Hmm," murmured Sam, around a bite of cucumber sandwich. "The New Orleans streetcars are the oldest continuously running streetcar system in the world."

"Well, I hope you will have a ride for me," Jillian said wistfully.

The two friends sat in companionable silence for a few minutes.

"Have you called home recently?" Jillian broached tentatively.

"Three months ago for Tasha's birthday." Sam sighed. She had called her sister to wish her happy birthday, hoping that things might have changed.

Her sister, hearing her voice and happy wishes, had wordlessly handed the telephone receiver to her husband, Michael, and fled the room. Through the phone, Sam could hear the panicked steps on the hardwood floors.

"Damn it, Samantha," Michael whispered, "I thought we had agreed that you weren't going to call here anymore."

"No, we didn't agree, Michael. You told me that it would be best if I didn't. I was hoping that she had had a change of heart."

"She just hears your name and she goes into a panic. Your voice puts her over the edge. For the love of God, Sam. Don't call anymore."

"I take it your call to your sister didn't go as you hoped?" Jillian asked, bringing Sam back to the present. At Sam's shake of her head, Jillian continued. "Is there any news on the case?" She knew Sam called the detective that was in charge of Justin's case every six months.

"No. Sometimes I think as a journalist if only I could interview all the witnesses, I could find a lead and bring the killer or killers to justice. But there are no witnesses."

Jillian nodded. Tristan had disappeared from the fenced-in outdoor space of his daycare. He was there one minute and then gone the next. No one had seen anything. Or anyone. The next time Justin was seen, he was a lifeless boy wrapped in a dirty blanket on the floor of a stolen van. No usable prints were found. No one had seen anything. Or if they had, they weren't talking.

"Do you think the case will ever be solved?" asked Jillian.

"Not unless someone involved confesses. Or they tell the wrong person in confidence and that person comes forward."

Sam sighed. "I should print out my boarding passes for tomorrow. Can I use your office printer so I don't have to drag out my portable?"

"Sure – you know where everything is."

Jillian sat with her tea while her friend sped into the office off the living room. *Now, when will that nightmare end?* She thought.

Down the hallway, Sam printed off her boarding passes for her economy seats. Air Canada 5738 to Denver, Air Canada 5509 Denver to New Orleans, Seats 8A and 10B respectively.

Economy, she grimaced. She thought for a moment about the long flight and the few months of her life when she had flown first class and thought nothing of it. She would stay at hotels like the Hotel Monteleone, not for a few days like Lauren but for weeks at a time.

Then she shook her head. No regrets. No regrets.

CHAPTER THIRTY-EIGHT

Daniel printed off his flight boarding passes for the next day's flights: AC 5738 3A, Business class to Denver.

He was booked into the Hotel Monteleone, the same hotel as Lauren.

He hadn't called her. He thought she might put him off. He hadn't told Rupert that he was going either. Rupert might have insisted on coming with him.

He would call her when he checked in to the Monteleone to see if she wanted to go down to the hotel bar for a drink.

He just didn't want to wait till the following morning if she was willing to sign the papers sooner. Only ten days left.

CHAPTER THIRTY-NINE

Over her shoulder, Lauren could hear the tour director of a small group of identically clothed tourists give information to her flock.

"In 1811, the first in a line of river steamboats left the dock at Pittsburgh to steam down the Ohio River to the Mississippi and on to New Orleans.

"For most of the 19th century and part of the early 20th century, trade on the Mississippi River was dominated by paddle-wheel steamboats. Their use saw rapid economic development of towns up and down the river thanks to increased trade in agricultural and commodity products.

"Most steamboats were destroyed by boiler explosions or fires, and many sank in the river, some to be covered over by silt as the river changed course.

"But do not be concerned," said the tourist guide slowly and loudly at the rumble of concern from her flock, "the Natchez, whose hospitality you are enjoying today, has a modern day boiler and fire suppression system to ensure your safety."

Trying to ignore the tour guides and their rehearsed speeches, Lauren passed a $20 bill to the girl in the ticket booth. "Ya'll have a good time," she drawled as she handed Lauren back her change.

With a mighty blast of its horn, the Natchez, set sail and Lauren could feel the breeze of the river lift her hair and cool the back of her neck.

What an odd term, Lauren thought. The Natchez had no sails, only engines and a paddle wheel at the back. It should be 'sets paddle,' not 'sets sail.'

She laughed at her own ridiculousness, before sobering up as a thought about the tough couple of days ahead entered her mind.

It will be fine. I will be fine, she told herself.

Day Eleven

New Orleans

Pan Roasted Magret Duck Breast
Caramelized Clementines, Wild Rice Pilaf,
Marsala Gastrique

Or

Cedar Springs Lamb Noisette
Mediterranean Couscous, Tawny Port Reduction,
Smoked Goat Cheese

Or

Shellfish "Coo-be-yon"
Grilled Grouper, Gulf Coast Shrimp, Louisiana
Blue Crab, Diver Scallop, Creole Tomato-Fennel
Broth, Citrus Linguini

CHAPTER FORTY

Sam followed the winding snake of passengers boarding the Air Canada flight to Denver.

She balanced her passport, boarding pass and shawl in one hand as she struggled to keep her rolling laptop case that held her laptop and camera equipment from banging into the legs of the passenger walking behind and slightly beside her.

Coming around the corner to enter the plane, she and her fellow economy passengers began the business class economy class identification ritual. The economy passengers looked curiously at the business passengers.

Anyone I know? Anyone famous?

The business class passengers did the corresponding 'I don't see you' part of their ritual, while peeping occasionally over their papers and E-readers to ask themselves a similar question. *Do I see anyone I know?*

Sam had perfected the curiosity ritual down to a lightning

quick visual scan. She took in three women in business suits, one cuddly couple and four men immersed in the Globe and Mail. As one drew back to turn the broadsheet page, she was surprised to take in the good looks of Daniel Zackery occupying seat 3A. He was focused on the newspaper and not on other passengers and didn't make eye contact with her or any of the other passengers.

Now, that is interesting, she thought, continuing her way to her seat in 8A.

What could be so important that Daniel would be heading to Denver when his wife was still missing? This is getting more intriguing.

And possibly dangerous if he is really involved in his wife's disappearance, she reminded herself.

Pushing thoughts of Daniel Zackery aside, Sam attempted to distract herself with the touch screen in-flight entertainment system on the Airbus A-330. As the plane took off and accelerated to its cruising speed of 520 mph, she took deep breaths and slowly released her death grip on the seat arm rests.

The woman in the centre seat, said comfortingly, "You must not fly often. Don't worry, you'll be fine."

The intrepid travel writer who was afraid of takeoffs tried to smile back.

After a reasonably calm flight to Denver, punctuated only by small moments of turbulence on the final approach, the flight arrived on time.

Sam quickly made her way to her gate where she boarded the AC 5509 flight destined for Louis Armstrong Airport, New Orleans. Walking past business class, Sam was only slightly surprised to see Daniel sitting in 2A by the window.

Why would he be going to New Orleans? To talk to Lauren? Was Rupert there as well? This was beyond odd.

By the time the flight was descending into New Orleans, Sam had changed her plans. Over the past hour, her sense of unease had increased. She initially put it down to her flying issues, but this feeling was different. Although her friends were expecting her, no one would be meeting her at the airport. She would go by the Hotel Monteleone first to see Lauren and set her own mind to rest that all was well with the twin.

CHAPTER FORTY-ONE

Sam arrived at the Hotel Monteleone with her rolling laptop case and larger suitcase in tow. Leaving the larger piece with the bellman, she walked to the house phone and had the receptionist ring up to Lauren's room. There was no answer.

Taking out her cell phone, she called the number Lauren's assistant had given her. No answer either. *This might take a while,* she thought. *Might as well wait and catch her when she returned.* If it became too late, she promised herself, and there was no sign of Lauren, she would go along to her friend's house and try to connect with the twin in the morning.

Sam left the lobby and entered the Carousel Bar and Lounge, identifying a vacant seat at the revolving bar. The Carousel was made famous by many authors, including Ernest Hemingway. The twenty-four-seat circus carousel dated back to 1949 and went around once every fifteen minutes. In the center of the carousel, a bartender happily dispersed libations to his collection of circus-going revolving patrons.

Sam stepped on the revolving circle and ran her hand over the back of her chosen chair. It was painted with a picture of a lion. Each chair back was a different animal, she remembered from a previous visit. *Lions, elephants and tigers. Oh my!*

She looked up at the blue and gold canopy overhead. Jesters and oval mirrors surrounded by light bulbs. The characters were trimmed in green and autumn leaves and wore red and yellow frilled collars. *Were their smiles genuine or mocking as they looked beyond the carousel's imbibers to the drinkers in the lounge?* she thought fancifully. She joined the other customers sitting at the carousel and looked up into the inner canopy to the faces of painted winged cherubs. *Did the angels approve of the drinkers' dissipated ways?*

Sam sat down in her lion chair and debated her own choice of poison. The carousel revolved, ticking off the seconds, waiting for her to decide.

As her first revolution lined up with the open doorway to the lobby, Sam saw Lauren. Sam hopped off the revolving bar, giving the barman a Gallic shrug as if to say she had a better offer.

Swinging shopping bags from each hand, Lauren approached the front desk and asked for messages. The receptionist said, "Yes, from your sister. She has landed and she is at her hotel. Please meet her at the Roosevelt in the Sazerac Bar." The receptionist completed reading the message to Lauren and then said, "Just a moment, our reservation manager wishes a minute with you."

Sam was stunned. Although she was more than thirty feet from Lauren and the receptionist, Sam took in every word as she lip-read the movements of the receptionist's mouth.

She leaned against the doorway to the Carousel Bar. *Sister?*

Does that mean Kathleen? It must! She must be alive! What was happening?

"She stopped by," the manager was saying. "A charming lady as well. You certainly can see that you are related. I just wanted to let you know that we have available accommodation here at the moment if your sister wishes to move from the Roosevelt to the Monteleone."

Sam read his lips. Pulling back into the shadows, her mind reeled. *Why would Kathleen come to New Orleans? How could she have escaped through the net of immigration without her travel documents flagging the police? Why did Rupert and Daniel not know and Lauren did. What was this plot?*

Lauren was on the move. She left her shopping with the receptionist and dashed across the lobby and out the door.

Sam waited until Lauren jumped into a well-worn red and gold Alliance cab before stepping from the shadows of the doorway to grab the cab behind.

Her mind raced with what she knew about the twins, their husbands, and the possible motives.

CHAPTER FORTY-TWO

Daniel pulled up to the Hotel Monteleone and was about to alight when he saw Lauren dash out of the hotel and jump into a red and gold Alliance cab.

Should he follow her or just check in? he asked himself.

He was gathering his light bag to exit when he looked up in time to see Sam Anderson leave the shadows of the hotel doorway and flag a match to his own black and white American cab.

Damn it, what the hell is that writer doing here? Where are they both going? He instructed the cab driver to follow the cab ahead. Seeing the cab driver's hesitation, he urged him with the lie to "Follow it quick – that is my girlfriend! We were to meet for drinks and my flight was late and so now she has deserted me. Help me make it up to her!"

Motivated by the chance to play a part in matchmaking, the cab driver smiled and pulled back into the single moving line of traffic making its way down the narrow French Quarter street.

CHAPTER FORTY-THREE

Sam wanted to let Lauren meet with Kathleen before either of them saw her.

Daniel wanted to find out where Sam and Lauren were going and for what purpose.

The first two cabs let out their individual passengers at the Roosevelt.

The historical hotel was born in 1893 as the Grunewald and was renamed the Roosevelt in 1923 in honour of American President Teddy Roosevelt.

Its magnificence was lost on Daniel as he focused on the two women ahead of him.

In the evening dusk and from the shadows of his taxi, Daniel watched Lauren and Sam get out of their respective taxis and enter the Roosevelt.

Throwing cash at the cab driver, he grabbed his bag and followed them into the hotel. Half way down the magnificent lobby hall and on the left was the Sazerac Bar.

At the doorway to the Sazerac, Sam stopped. Standing just outside the door, she saw Lauren barrel forward with her customary energy that had been amiss for the past week.

A woman with short curly hair jumped up from the far booth and flung herself into Lauren's arms. From the door, Sam gasped and thought, "*Oh my God, it really is Kathleen!*"

She moved forward.

CHAPTER FORTY-FOUR

From behind her, Sam neither saw nor heard Daniel move into the same position she had been at a moment before.

Over Sam's retreating shoulder, Daniel saw Lauren and her dark haired mirror.

He jumped from the doorway and moved quickly back to the front door of the Roosevelt. He needed to think. At the hotel entrance, he jumped into the cab he just vacated and instructed the cab driver to return to the Hotel Monteleone.

"How could she do this to me," he railed in the back seat, drawing the driver's anxious attention. He thought to explain with another lie but then thought it was unnecessary. It wasn't any of the man's business.

Where has she been for the past week! Juneau? New Orleans? How did she fly here without her passport? That damn Lauren! She had to part of this!

Realizing that the twins had conspired against him in some

way, Daniel started to vibrate with anger. *What were they doing? Why would Kathleen hide from me? Was she planning on leaving me? Had she already left me? How does this affect the money?*

What about the equity loan on the life insurance policy? Now he could prove she was alive, that should go through and he could get the cash. *But wouldn't the five million be better?* he thought suddenly. *The police already believe she might be dead.*

No one knew that he was in New Orleans, not either of the twins nor Rupert. Nor did either of the twins know that he knew that Kathleen was alive.

At the front desk he left a written message for Lauren to ensure she received it. "Need to talk to you tomorrow. I am thinking of hiring a private detective but would like to talk to you first. Couldn't get a hold of you on the phone so flew down tonight."

In his room, Daniel paced the floor. Time was disappearing. He only had nine days left.

He scanned through the directory on his cell phone until he found the number of the fellow he had been less than pleased to see a couple of days ago in Joe Fortes. One of the boys.

"Tony, yes it's Daniel Zackery. Listen, Tony, I am down in New Orleans working on a little deal and the client insists on me picking up physical cash. This in New Orleans – carrying cash around is an invitation for trouble. Anyways I would feel better if I had a gun with me and I know you have friends everywhere. Is there someone down here that could set me up with a handgun? I only need it for two days. You know, how odd some investors can be. The more money they have, the more eccentric."

After listening to Tony's instructions, he said, "I'll wait for his call. Thanks Tony."

CHAPTER FORTY-FIVE

The Sazerac Bar was a long graceful room with walls of wood interrupted by four iconic murals and a vast mirror behind a bar made of African walnut. The two sisters breathed in the atmosphere and smiled at each other, holding hands tightly. Only now believing that the other was there and safe.

The wait for Lauren to arrive in the bar had been difficult for Kathleen. She had whiled away the time by enjoying the cool air around her and the quiet conversations in the banquettes to her right. Visitors would slip into the cool leather club chairs with a sigh, as if talking too loud would be too casual or disrespectful.

Two men sat at the bar itself, their shined dress leather shoes propped on the brass bar rail as they balanced on the tall stools. She could occasionally hear one of the four white jacketed bartenders explain to a bar patron how a specific cocktail was made. The bartender was now explaining the history and secret of the world's first mixed drink and the official cocktail of New

Orleans, The Sazerac. Apparently the key ingredients were Sazerac 6-year-old Rye Whiskey, Peychaud's Bitters and Sugar, all in a Herbsaint-rinsed glass.

Was it 2013 or was it 1913 at the dawn of the cocktail era? Kathleen thought. You could be confused by looking at the bar, the service and the uniforms.

Jazz played in the background, but it was as if it was coming from the four murals themselves. Kathleen tried to identify the characters in the iconic paintings on the walls of the bar. In the mural to the right of the bar mirror, was that the Duchess of Windsor and J.P. Morgan? He with a cigar and she with a fur-trimmed coat. Wouldn't it have been too warm to wear fur in New Orleans? Or was that just the way it was then?

But finally Lauren had come and she had tossed herself at her twin sister with all the longing for her confidant that she had held inside for the past week. They had never gone a day in their 33 years not talking to each other, even on their honeymoons. However, this was very serious business and they had decided that they needed to be silent until they could meet here.

"So where are we?' asked Lauren, meaning the process, not the location of their physical bodies.

"Everything is in place. Just waiting for you to sign a couple of documents and then I will scan and email everything. Once we have a copy of the transfer of funds, I will approach Daniel and tell him what we have done."

"What have you done, Kathleen?"

The two women swung around at Sam's question. They had been so caught up with each other that Sam's presence had been unnoticed.

"Busted." Lauren cried.

"All for good reasons, though," Kathleen added, holding her hands up palm outwards.

Sam sat in the accompanying club chair to the half circle booth. "I am all ears."

Lauren looked at Kathleen.

"No point in not telling her at this point. We are almost done and she has seen you," Lauren coaxed.

Kathleen nodded.

"I am sure you have a good reason why. But first I want to know how you did it. How did you get off the ship? How did you get into the country?" asked Sam.

Kathleen began the tale. "When we left the ship in Juneau, Lauren and I were wearing identical jackets."

"Except hers was navy with ivory lining and mine was ivory with navy lining," interrupted Lauren.

"That's right, I remember that," Sam nodded. "Where did you go after the Mendenhall glacier?"

"I took a taxi to the mall."

"You went shopping!"

"Exactly, I bought hair dye, scissors, toiletries, underwear, several sets of pajamas, a sweatshirt, a suitcase, five books, fruit and microwaveable frozen dinners."

"Then where did you go?"

"I checked into the Travelodge at the Juneau airport using the name Jen Williams and using Lauren's credit card and driver's license."

"Lauren Jennifer Williams. Jen Williams. Lauren Williams. It is different enough that if the police had had publicized that Barbra Zackery has a sister named Lauren Williams, no one would question that. You would also have to have had a credit card to check in to the hotel," Sam nodded.

"So Jen Williams held up for five days in a hotel. I used the in-house launderette to wash the new clothes. I cut and coloured my own hair. I told the front desk that I was under the weather and each time they came in to straighten the room and take out the garbage, I stayed in the washroom and tossed out the used towels in exchange for the fresh ones they left. I had minimum contact in case my face was all over the news. The hotel room had a mini fridge and a microwave so, except for using the business centre in the middle of the night, I didn't need to leave the room until yesterday afternoon when I flew from Juneau to Seattle."

"And then Seattle to New Orleans today," Sam completed.

"Yes."

"So why did you stay in Juneau so long. Why not leave right away?"

"She needed my passport!" Lauren jumped in. "I flew to New Orleans and then the next day I couriered my passport to Jen Williams at the Travelodge. Kathleen, using my identification, received it the following morning and flew to Seattle that afternoon. That was the quickest we could turn it around."

"Also," Kathleen added, "we wanted to ensure that it was possible that Lauren could physically have flown from New Orleans back to Juneau in time for me to fly as her back to New Orleans. As it was, I sailed right through security and arrived here without question."

Sam thought about that for a moment. "How did you get off the ship?"

"I walked off with the rest of the passengers at Juneau the fourth morning of the cruise."

"But how did you... Oh I see... Lauren played the part of both of you when she re-boarded. She used both of your cruise ID cards to show that you both had re-boarded."

Lauren's jaw dropped. "How did you figure that out?"

Sam smiled, remembering her own clumsiness at the gangway. "I know how it could be done, but how did you manage it?"

Lauren was bubbling over with her moment to explain her part in the great escape. "I have to tell you first this was not my idea and I was quite nervous even scared really. Who knows what the ship security would do to me if I was caught?"

"Lauren?" Kathleen prompted.

"Back to the reversible jacket. I waited till a large crowd was coming to the re-entry point. When I re-boarded, I was scanned in as myself. Just at that point, I fumbled my card and dropped it. In the crowd, I turned around as if to talk to someone and kicked the card with my foot. I quickly worked my way around the first corner. Then I flipped my coat inside out. I stuck my hair under the hat that Kathleen handed to me before she got into the taxi at the Mendenhall Glacier.

"I didn't have time to put my hair up into a French roll and my bangs would have hung done anyways. By reversing my coat and tucking up my hair in Kathleen's hat, I would pass if they had security video.

"Then I checked in again, using Kathleen's cruise ID card, making sure I used one of the other security lines to board and kept my face turned away from the first guard.

"So that is what George saw that day. Your conversion."

"Exactly."

"What?" asked Kathleen.

"George asked me if it was me or you he saw in the gangway going back to the ship in Juneau that afternoon."

"Did he tell the security or police?" Kathleen asked, a panicked look coming over her face.

"No he didn't," Sam answered.

"How do you know?"

"George is a retired cop and he and I bonded over this mystery," Sam said trying to calm Kathleen.

"What mystery?" Kathleen asked.

"The missing Kathleen, of course," Sam answered.

CHAPTER FORTY-SIX

"Is he going to be a problem, do you think?" Kathleen asked Sam.

"Don't worry about George. He is on your side in all this, I'm certain. Okay, now tell me the why."

The two sisters looked at each other

"It is tough to find out you married a liar," Kathleen began.

"I had five solid days to think about my life, my marriage and the money. I was in a hotel room alone for five days to think. I don't think he ever loved me. If it wasn't for the money, I don't think I would have attracted him. If I was just an accountant who worked at a charity for a salary as my only asset and financial security, I would have been overlooked by Daniel. When we began dating, he said that we were a perfect match." She laughed humourlessly. "I didn't know that the perfect match was him and the millions."

Lauren leaned closer and put her arm around her sister.

"Damn bastard," she whispered.

Sam watched the love between the two sisters and thought about her own long term connection for her sister, recently destroyed. She shook her head to get back to the moment.

"From the moment we became engaged, he started to push for us to move the investments to his boutique firm. I had so many problems with that. One a smaller firm is riskier. There is no 'too big to fail' provisions. Secondly, I felt it was too close to home. I know that sounds funny. It is our money, technically. He is my husband. Lauren and I work for the charity. I just wanted more of an arms-length relationship with the investment managers. In case things go, as Rupert would say, all pear-shaped. I wanted to make sure I didn't lose my marriage over it. Ha. Now that's rather funny, isn't it?

"I was slowly exercising the plan that Lauren and I decided upon last year. I kept telling Daniel that we were thinking of making a change. And that is true. Just not to his firm and control. The longer I took, the more... the more... I don't know... aggressive he became. Then, he started being rough with me and I had had enough.

"I mentioned a separation and he really scared me, saying he would never let me go. Finally, the first day on the ship, I was flipping through his briefcase looking for some writing paper and I found a copy of my will and my life insurance policy. I think for a moment my heart stopped. Certainly my breathing did.

"I knew I was running out of time. We had started the process but that day I realized that Daniel would be furious about us giving away the money. When I found my will and life insurance documents in his luggage while on the cruise, I knew that I needed to take action fast."

"The bastard!" Lauren was rubbing her sister's arm in comfort, but now thumped her fist on the bar table.

For a moment the three women thought about the significance of the will and life insurance policy.

"Along with those documents, he even brought a set of papers for me to sign to make his firm the investment managers for the money. Even on a cruise, a holiday, he said, it was all about the money. If it wasn't for the money...."

"Get it all out honey. You might feel better." Lauren said.

"I will feel better when I see confirmation of the transfer of funds and final documents signed and processed."

Lauren looked up at Sam. "We decided the best thing to do was to get rid of the money. We have started a private foundation and are surrendering the millions to it to invest and distribute to registered charities according to its constitution. We have a fair bit of control of which type of charities are supported, but we have pretty much surrendered permanent control."

"You probably think we are insane," Kathleen laughed.

"Actually, I don't." Sam said. In fact, not only was it what she would have done. It was what she had done.

CHAPTER FORTY-SEVEN

The three women moved upstairs to Kathleen's room to complete the final steps of the plan, using Sam's laptop, her mini scanner/printer and the hotel Wi-Fi internet. Kathleen had done everything she could with the business centre at the Travelodge but she had needed Lauren's signature and the documents witnessed. Sam was pleased to play that role.

Once the documents were signed, witnessed, scanned and emailed to the proper authorities, Lauren asked, "Don't you think we need a celebration drink?"

Leaving Sam's rolling bag in Kathleen's room, they went back down to the Sazerac Bar. They sat at the bar and all ordered a glass of wine.

"It is a good thing that you are doing this now." Sam said, swirling the remaining red wine in her glass.

"Why?" the twins asked at the same time. They smiled at each other, reminding Sam that although they couldn't be any different in personality they were still twins.

"I saw Daniel on the plane from Vancouver to Denver and Denver to New Orleans."

Kathleen and Lauren gasped in unison.

"Yes, it is good that it is done," Lauren breathed out in a whoosh, and then finished her glass of wine.

CHAPTER FORTY-EIGHT

Two hours after he had first made the call to Tony, Daniel answered the knock at his hotel door. He had gone to an instant bank machine to take out his daily maximum of $1000 cash. The cash was in a Hotel Monteleone envelope in the desk drawer.

Ten minutes later, the envelope was gone and he was in possession of a holster, a wet silencer and a semi-automatic .40 calibre Glock Gen4 with a 15 round clip of .40 calibre 180-grain bullets.

Tony's friend had explained that the wet silencer was more effective than a dry silencer at muffling the sound. Any silencer cools the exhaust gases when a bullet is fired and the cooling of the exhaust gasses is what muffles the sound. A wet silencer, thanks to a wetting agent and nitrogen spray, cools the gases more effectively and therefore reduces sound even further. Tony's friend had already applied the wetting agent to make it easy for Daniel if and when Daniel needed to fire the Glock.

To reduce the FRP or first round pop when the very first shot was fired, Daniel was told he needed to spray nitrogen from a small aerosol container into the end of the barrel and put a small piece of masking tape over the end of the barrel. This task would have to be done within fifteen minutes before taking the first shot.

Playing the part of the concerned possible victim, Daniel had asked, "How do I know when I may be attacked? I won't have time to spray the nitrogen?"

Tony's friend had smiled as he left the hotel room, "It has been my experience that anyone who needs a silencer has a plan to address that issue."

Daniel stroked the shiny black barrel with his index finger. *Am I really going to use this?*

He put on the shoulder holster and then shrugged into his suit jacket. He slid the gun into the holster pocket. The silencer, the nitrogen and the tape that Tony's friend had helpfully supplied were deposited into his suit pocket.

He left the hotel and took a taxi back to the Roosevelt.

CHAPTER FORTY-NINE

Daniel entered the Sazerac Bar on the hopes that the three women were still in the quiet bar. There was more evening traffic than before, but no sign of any of the three.

He sat at the bar in the chair closest to the banquette he had seen Lauren and Kathleen sitting at.

"What can I get you sir?" asked the bartender.

Daniel put a confused look on his face. "Well I was meeting some friends here and it looks like I am too early or too late. If I missed them, I should go and try to track them down."

"What did they look like?"

Daniel struggled to remember Sam's hair colour. "Three gals – one redhead, one blonde and one brunette. They said they would be in a booth but I don't see them."

"Well you are in luck, sir. They did meet up here and then left for a bit and then came back and sat at the bar. The redhead said that there was no need for them to sit here in the hotel when

New Orleans is calling. She had been to town before, but I think the other two were new to New Orleans."

"Do you know where they headed to?"

"The blonde wanted to experience some local music and I suggested going down to Frenchman street for some music. The redhead said their first stop should be the Spotted Cat."

"Is that on Frenchmen street?"

"Yes, if you catch a cab, any driver will know it."

Daniel put on a smile and placed a $20 bill on the counter. "Thanks for that. You saved me a lot of time trying to track them down."

CHAPTER FIFTY

Jazz is considered one of America's only original art forms but Sam always found it interesting that it was born in a city that was so unlike the core of America. Prior to the Louisiana Purchase in 1803, the New Orleans culture was comprised of French, American Indian, Spanish, and West African people. African dance and drumming was heard and seen as early as the 1780s when African Americans socialized on Sundays in the area now known as Congo Square.

After Louisiana joined the United States of America as the 18th state, it was flooded by Americans, enslaved Africans, and immigrants from Germany, Haiti, and Italy. This mosaic and history was fertile ground for the beginning of such a unique sound. New Orleans in the very early 1900s became a vibrant center for theater, vaudeville, music publishing houses, parades, and dance clubs.

Although the music of New Orleans has spread to all areas

of the country and some would say around the world, Sam felt a special something sitting in one of the clubs off the tourist track listening to a local band or singer. The Spotted Cat was one of her favourite places.

The Spotted Cat Music Club sported green paint on the walls and ceiling, a roughed up bar running the length of the long and narrow room, mismatched bar stools, a couple of high top tables and a ten by eight stage to the right of the front doors.

The air conditioning pumped out coolish air into the packed room and warmed slightly when the three women entered through the swinging doors, bringing a puff of the warmer humid outside air with them.

There was standing room only when they entered so they found a piece of wall to lean against and listened to the singer. Sam elbowed her way to the bar and brought back three gin and tonics. The music was free, but for the fee of buying one drink per set.

Handing the sisters their drinks, Sam leaned against her space on the wall.

The singer's raspy, gravelly voice was accompanied by a stand-up bass and a piano. Sam smiled at the sign above the piano with its misspelled message that read "No drinks or drunks on the pianee." It had been there her last visit and its presence gave her a welcoming feeling.

As the evening evolved, Lauren and Kathleen saw the pattern. When a group ended its set, they circulated with a hat giving the patrons an opportunity to tip them for their efforts and talent and buy their recorded CD for a mere $10 or $15. Then, many patrons left for a cigarette, food, or another venue. It was that exact moment when the dash was made by the remainder of the standing patrons for the vacant stools and high tops. By the second set break, Lauren had scored them a high top table and they all sat.

CHAPTER FIFTY-ONE

During the break between the next sets, Lauren looked at the art around the room by the local artist, Belladonna.

"I like that," she said and began to wander around the room looking at the many pieces. Stopping at a spot where art cards gave background on the artist she took one from the plastic holder and slowly turned to hear the returning singer. She sounded like she was giving birth through the song and the notes compelled Lauren to just lean against the door and experience the moment.

Opening her eyes, she looked out the window. For a moment she thought she recognized Daniel. She blinked and looked again. If he was there, he was now lost into the crowd.

If he was here outside the Spotted Cat, it was a coincidence. No one but she, Kathleen and Sam knew that they had been at the Roosevelt and they had come directly here from there. But it would be a good idea for them to leave soon none-the-less. No point risking any contact until they had everything ready.

CHAPTER FIFTY-TWO

Sam and the twins exited the Spotted Cat, each with a ten-dollar CD in hand.

As Lauren and Kathleen waved at a cab half way down the block, Sam's attention was drawn to the crowd across the street in front of another music venue, the Snug Harbor.

She thought she saw Daniel. He separated himself for a moment and lifted his arm. For a moment, she thought he was about to wave, but realized that his right hand and arm were not moving back and forth in a waving motion. His right arm was bent at the elbow with the forearm directly extended in their direction and in his hand was a black....

"Shit!" she shouted, throwing herself against Kathleen and Lauren. She thought she heard two little pops but was quickly distracted by massive pain and her diving descent down to the sidewalk.

CHAPTER FIFTY-THREE

Daniel moved his hand down quickly and stepped back into the crowd. He tucked the gun into the copy of the daily Times Picayune, New Orleans daily newspaper, that he carried in his left hand.

Several people across the street saw the women fall down and a crowd began to form.

Curiosity seekers from his side of the street ran across the street to see what the fuss was all about. There was a cluster of people growing around the three across the street.

He slipped into the shadows. He didn't want anyone recognizing him or catching him in an IPhone picture or video. But he had to wait until he knew.

A man with his arm around a crying woman ran back across the street and stopped within three feet of Daniel.

"What happened over there?" he asked, nodding towards the crowd. He kept his voice interested but neutral, even though inside he was quaking. He registered the need for presenting a calm demeanour. *I am doing extremely well,* he congratulated himself. *I shot her. I just shot my wife!*

"I think there was a drive by shooting. It looks like two women are dead over there. Lots of blood. What a terrible way to end our holiday."

"Has someone called the police or an ambulance?" he asked the tourist.

"I think so but look at this traffic! I don't think a cop car or ambulance will get here any time soon. I don't know if it will matter if they could. Neither of them is moving. Someone said that they are both dead. My wife didn't want to get too close."

"As soon as I saw all the blood in that woman's curly black hair, I had to turn away," his wife whispered.

"Honey," she said looking up to her husband's face, "I think I am going to be sick."

"Excuse us" the man said, wheeling his wife away from the crowd just in time for her to vomit over the hood of a red rental car parked at the curb.

Daniel stepped back quickly and began to walk away from the crowds and down the first side street. He removed the silencer and pocketed it. He put the gun back into the shoulder holster and buttoned his suit jacket in spite of the humid heat. He tossed the newspaper onto the street and hailed a cab.

CHAPTER FIFTY-FOUR

"Rupert, we were shot at. I think it might have been Daniel," Lauren said into her cell phone.

The three women were in Kathleen's room at the Roosevelt. The room Kathleen had rented until she reconnected with Lauren had been transformed into a fortress against known and unknown forces.

The reality of the events of the evening had been too much for Lauren and she had to reach out to her husband to find comfort.

"What! Are you hurt? Why would he shoot at you? He must be insane! This doesn't make any sense!" Rupert's voice was clearly heard by the other occupants in the room.

"No, no, none of us are hurt."

"Who is us?" he asked.

"Kathleen, Sam and me." Lauren immediately slapped her hand across her mouth. But the words were already out. For a moment in her state of anxiety, Lauren forgot the script.

"Kathleen? You found Kathleen! Lauren, oh Lauren I am so glad." Rupert was overcome with worry, happiness and relief.

"Lauren?"

"It's very complicated, Rupert. It will be all straightened and finished by early afternoon. We are going to meet with Daniel tomorrow for lunch at noon at Commander's Palace and tell him that we are finished with him."

"What are you talking about? Have you lost your mind?! If he did this terrible thing, I don't want you to go near him!"

"We are meeting him for lunch and we are telling him that Kathleen is divorcing him, that she has changed her life insurance from him as beneficiary and that we are giving all the millions away and he will never have control over them."

"You are giving the millions away?"

"To a foundation that will manage them and donate to charities." Lauren paused.

"Are you upset about that" she asked in a whisper, wondering if her marriage was connected to the millions in some way as well. She and Rupert had married before the twins had inherited, but Rupert had always known about the money and that it would one day be hers. How much did the millions matter to her marriage?

"Am I upset about that?" Rupert laughed. "No darling, I am not upset about that one bit."

CHAPTER FIFTY-FIVE

Sam took the prescription painkiller from Kathleen and swallowed it down with a glass of champagne.

"Don't look at me like that," she accused, pointing at the disapproving scowl on Kathleen's face. "You weren't shot twice today."

The two bullets released from Daniel's gun had both hit Sam as she threw herself across Kathleen and Lauren. One had grazed her upper arm, hitting the cephalic vein and releasing a considerable amount of blood. The second had grazed her temple, releasing blood that had flowed across her face. The vast amount of Sam's shed blood had been deposited on Kathleen's face, hair and blouse as Sam fell towards her, taking them both down to the sidewalk. The collision of the cement with Kathleen's head knocked her out cold for several minutes.

Although there had been considerable blood and initially Sam had been stunned and Kathleen unconscious, the two women were actually nowhere near meeting their maker. The quick thinking of a local resident drew medical assistance from the firehouse at the end of the block and Sam and Kathleen were soon on their way to hospital for attention. Although Sam had lost blood, the gunshot was through the fleshy part of her upper arm and had missed the bone. The graze on her forehead had only required three stiches. Two hours after the shooting the three were on the way back to the hotel.

Sam reclined on Kathleen's bed at the Roosevelt. She rolled up the sleeves of Kathleen's pajamas. She had called her friend to tell her she would be seeing her the following day. Lauren had called the Hotel Monteleone and the bellman was sending over the rolling suitcase Sam had left with him earlier. All three women had showered to remove the blood and dishevelment of the evening and were dressed in matching hotel robes.

Sam looked at her watch, five minutes past three.

What a bizarre day today has been, she thought. Started out nicely with a friendly pat down at security at the Vancouver airport, a mediocre meal at the Denver airport, the unveiling of the Kathleen mystery, an hour of the fabulous music of Meschiya Lake and the Little Big Horns at the Spotted Cat, a bullet to the head and one to the arm and now champagne and painkillers.

She sat up suddenly, holding steady to let the pain settle when the movement jarred her head. "Call room service! I haven't had a proper meal since this morning. And I am in New Orleans for crying out loud!"

CHAPTER FIFTY-SIX

Daniel put the chain on the lock of his hotel door as if protecting himself from the police that hadn't come to the scene. *Had someone seen him? What the hell was he thinking?*

Killing Kathleen in a city with one of the highest crime rates in America during a crowded night in an area outside of the general tourist area was absolute luck. However, would Lauren think that his presence was tied to Kathleen's shooting?

He looked down at the instructions for the disposal of the gun left by Tony's friend. In a shopping bag was a roll of wrapping paper, a business card with just a number and a name, scissors, scotch tape, bubble wrap and an empty box for New Orleans favourite candy, pralines.

He was to remove the silencer from the end of the gun, wrap the silencer, the holder, unused ammunition and the gun in the bubble wrap, place the items in the praline box, tape the box shut, and then wrap the box with the wrapping paper. He was then to call the number on the card, telling whoever answered that the gift was ready. Then he was to put the wrapped box in the shopping bag, leave it with the concierge for a courier to pick it up and deliver it to the gentlemen at the address on the card.

The gentleman who had left the gun had told him to be unconcerned if for some reason the gun was discharged. He would clean it when it was returned. The thousand dollars included the cleaning and dealing with any discharged ammunition issues, as he termed it.

Daniel looked at the shopping bag and back to the gun. Maybe he would hold on to it for another day or so.

Day Twelve

New Orleans

The New Yorker
Norwegian Smoked Salmon, Toasted Bagel,
Cream Cheese, Boiled Egg, Capers, Red Onion,
Local Tomato

Or

The Southern Eggs Benedict with Poached eggs,
Country Ham, Buttermilk Biscuits,
Hollandaise Sauce, and Stone Ground Grits

Or

Eggs Tchoupitoulas with Two Basted Eggs,
Boudin Blanc, Fried Green Tomato

CHAPTER FIFTY-SEVEN

The twins had slept together on the pull out couch in the living room area of the large hotel room. Sam had been given the bed. "You did save our lives, after all," Lauren insisted when Sam went to get up and surrender the king sized sea of comfort.

Kathleen put a cup of coffee on the end table. She pulled back the drapes to the morning sunshine. Turning back to the sleeping Sam, she picked up the room service menu and waved it under Sam's nose as if the smell of the paper alone would wake her.

"Sam, time to order room service," she whispered. Slowly she began to read selections in a sensuous voice. "The New Yorker with Norwegian Smoked Salmon, Toasted Bagel, Cream Cheese, Boiled Egg, Capers, Red Onion, Local Tomato. The Southern Eggs Benedict with Poached eggs, Country Ham, Buttermilk Biscuits, Hollandaise Sauce, and Stone Ground Grits. Eggs Tcha Tcha," Kathleen struggled with the word.

"Tchoupitoulas," Sam said from under the covers.

"Eggs Tchoupitoulas with Two Basted Eggs, Boudin Blanc, Fried Green Tomato, and Country Biscuit," Kathleen continued.

"Sam, please tell me you are hungry," Lauren said from the doorway. "Then I'll know you're okay."

"The eggs benedict and ask for extra hollandaise sauce," came the voice from the covers. "Any coffee?"

"Beside you on the table," Kathleen said, leaving Sam to wake up.

The room service porter arrived and took with him the evidence of the Shellfish Coo-be-yon late night meal of Grilled Grouper, Gulf Coast Shrimp, Louisiana Blue Crab, Diver Scallop, Creole Tomato-Fennel Broth, and Citrus Linguini.

Sam took two painkillers with her pineapple juice and turned to the lovely set room service cart that transformed into a small and convenient dining table. She pulled up a chair and smiled.

"When are we meeting Daniel?" she asked, shaking out a linen napkin and placing it on her lap.

When Lauren had called over the evening before regarding Sam's luggage, the receptionist had told her that there was a message from a Mr. Zackery. She had the receptionist read the note from Daniel and then left a message herself. She had told Daniel that she would meet him the next day at noon for lunch at Commander's Palace. The fact that the famous restaurant was across from a famous cemetery somehow seemed apropos.

"Please also tell him that I have had a horrible and tragic day, am all alone and need his help." Lauren asked the receptionist to read the message back to her. "Yes, that will do" she said before breaking the connection.

"I told Rupert last night that I would call him as soon as we get back from meeting with Daniel," Lauren added.

They ate in quiet companionship until all that was left to consume was half a pot of coffee. Sitting back in her seat, Sam sighed.

"I don't think I have ever met anyone who so enjoys good food," Lauren said, shaking her head at Sam.

"Wonderful food is indeed one of life's great pleasures," Sam laughed and then quickly grimaced when the stitches above her right eye pulled. "Ouch!"

The sisters looked at each other in mutual guilt.

"Stop it you two! It was his fault, not yours. He will get his just desserts. I have a call to make to help towards that end. But before that, I think we should call George."

"Why!" both sisters cried.

"He will know the ins and outs of what we need to do legally. We need to figure out exactly what the possible consequences are of the various identity switches you two engaged in."

The twins looked at each other and nodded. The in-concert communication between the two sisters both amused and saddened Sam. She remembered when she and her sister, Tasha, communicated just with a look.

CHAPTER FIFTY-EIGHT

"Hello George. It is Sam Anderson here." The two sisters were hearing only Sam's side of the conversation. "Yes, I'm fine. I am in the lovely city of New Orleans. Yes, you should come visit one day. Yes, the food is fantastic. George, we need your help. I am going to put you on speaker phone."

Sam clicked the button for speaker and placed her cell phone on the coffee table where all three women could talk and listen.

"George we need your help. I am sitting her with Lauren Williams and Kathleen Zackery."

"Kathleen Zackery! Where did she come from?"

Kathleen smiled and answered, "Hi, George. Nice to hear your voice."

"Kathleen, are you all right?!"

"Yes I am fine. Sam is a little worse for wear. She took two bullets for me last night."

"From Daniel?"

"How did you know?"

"Only logical conclusion."

Sam broke into the conversation. "George, let me bring you up to date."

After Sam completed the tale, filling in the many details that George would want to know, he had several questions.

"Kathleen, why did you decide to disappear from the ship? You explained how you did it, but what gave you the idea to try it in the first place?

"The Costa Concordia."

"The ship that sank off Italy a year or so ago?"

"That's the one. It hit rocks off a little island. The ship did not have a safety drill, and the hubris of the captain lead to fatalities. The captain did not call the coast guard and was in fact one of the first off the ship.

"As I watched the news about that cruise ship, I wondered how would they know who was dead or alive. How would they know if someone just... left.

"Shortly after thinking about the possible mystery of identifying people from the ship, one of the missing travellers appeared. She had swam to the shore, had been helped by islanders and then found her own way back to her home country of Germany. She just... left.

"When I found the documents in Daniel's briefcase that first day at sea, the German woman came to my mind. What if I just left?"

"Then what did you do?"

"I went on-line while at the Juneau hotel to move ahead our schedule for finalizing the creation of our new foundation.

Prior to the cruise, we had done a fair bit of work to put together and get approval of the various pieces of paperwork needed to convert the millions into a foundation.

"While in Juneau, I used the hotel business centre to complete the paperwork and once the papers were approved, they were couriered to our hotel here in New Orleans. Yesterday afternoon, once Lauren arrived, we signed, scanned and sent the necessary documents. This morning I received the confirmation that all the money has been transferred to the new foundation. I also have called my lawyer and told him to redraft my will and to notify the life insurance company of my transfer of beneficiary for my life insurance."

"From Daniel to...? George asked.

"To Sam and Lauren."

"What?" Sam said, "That's crazy."

"Sam," Kathleen said slowly. "I would be dead right now except for you. Those bullets were real and you moved in front of me. If anyone is crazy it is you."

"Well, we will talk about this later," Sam warned and went back to George.

"George, what are the consequences of their actions."

"It is not illegal, just disrespectful perhaps, to walk off a cruise ship without alerting security. It is not illegal to go on a walkabout and to return. Technically, it was Daniel who raised the hue and cry about Kathleen's disappearance however he did that in good faith, meaning, he really thought something had gone amiss. There may be a charge from the cruise ship regarding a nuisance or mischief charge, relating to the cost of security to look for you on board. However, as they are registered in Panama, that would be difficult for them to do.

"Lauren," he continued, "I am assuming Kathleen used your credit cards, identification and passport all with your permission?"

At Lauren's agreement, he continued, "So, Kathleen, you did fly across an international border using identification that was not yours, but it was neither false, nor stolen. And as you flew Juneau-Seattle-New Orleans, an argument could be made that there were no international borders crossed. You left the ship in the United States and you remained in American territory. So you have flown, Kathleen, using identification that is not your own within one country.

"Lauren, did you at any time give false witness to police officers or security officers?"

"No, but they never asked me directly if I knew what had happened to Kathleen or where she was. Only details about what had happened in Juneau before I returned to the ship. I was never put in a position where I had to bear false witness."

"Kathleen, you said you dyed your hair black by yourself?"

"Yes, it would have been too big a risk to go to a salon in Juneau. If the police had taken the situation more seriously, my face would have been everywhere.

"It worked in our favour that kidnapping is very rare and that no one believed that I was depressed enough to jump overboard. I think the police in Alaska and the security aboard the ship simply thought I had run away – which is exactly what I did," Kathleen admitted.

"Get yourself to a salon then and dye your colour back to match your passport picture before you try to fly. If you can't access your passport to get back into Canada, go to the closest Canadian consulate office and they will get you straightened out."

"George," Sam asked, "are you saying you think they are off the hook?"

"I think if anything comes up, use the danger that you believe Daniel posed. That should give you more legal options."

"Thanks George, you have really taken away my worry," said Lauren.

"Well I am a little worried about the three of you meeting Daniel for lunch at Commander's Palace. If he was the one who shot Sam, he is more dangerous than you are taking him as."

"I think he was the one," Lauren confirmed. "We think he thought that if Kathleen was dead, he would get the life insurance. We are assuming that he thinks he was successful last night with the shooting. He is not going to bring a gun to a restaurant at noon, not when he thinks that I am now willing to do what Kathleen wouldn't."

"I still don't like it. I don't like that you haven't called the police about him shooting Sam last night. However," he paused, "we don't know where he got the gun from and if that person is connected in some way to someone in authority. New Orleans is a strange town that way. But I just don't like it one bit. Call me as soon as it is over. I mean that. Don't leave me hanging, worrying. Promise, right now!"

"We promise," they all three said at the same time.

CHAPTER FIFTY-NINE

First thing after getting Lauren's message regarding lunch, Daniel rang four contacts in New Orleans, anxious to set up his justification for the trip. He came to see his sister-in-law and to do a little business.

He organized a morning meeting before he headed out to meet Lauren at the Commander's Palace and a meeting at three to round out his alibi after lunch.

He practiced his sympathetic expression in the mirror over the hotel room bathroom sink. He expected that Lauren would tell him about Kathleen being killed by a drive-by shooter and needing his help. He would act surprised that Kathleen had been found and play the wounded husband of a wife who had over-imagined his anger and had deserted their marriage. He thought he could find some tears if necessary.

Soon all would be well. Lauren was not the clear thinker that Kathleen was. She would be easily moved. Once Rupert started working on her, it wouldn't be any time before the millions were under his control. And, he rubbed his hands, he would also have the life insurance money.

Finally, and just in time to pay off the boys and get back into their good graces. *Life was looking up!*

CHAPTER SIXTY

Sam took another pain killer and then called her editor at Global Perspectives. They usually communicated by email and, in fact, Sam had never spoken directly to him.

When the line was picked up, a voice only said, "This better be good."

"Christopher?" Sam asked.

"Yes, again, this better be good."

Sam thought for a moment that his voice sounded like butter, no maple syrup, molasses maybe. She shook herself and got to the point. "This is Sam Anderson and do I have a story for you."

"You usually email me. I prefer it."

Sexy voice or not, Sam was having a tough couple of days. "Well I was shot twice in the past twelve hours so perhaps you could cut me some slack," she barked back.

CHAPTER SIXTY-ONE

Lauren sat in the booth at Commander's Palace alone. The plan was for Daniel to come in and sit down beside her. She was to hand him the papers and one minute later, Sam and Kathleen would come into the room and sit down. They would box him in, Kathleen beside Lauren and Sam beside Daniel.

Lauren hoped there wouldn't be any screaming. Restaurant fights are really embarrassing. She really thought nothing beyond that could occur. They were in a public place after all. What could Daniel do?

Sam had told her that she hoped that all could be settled with Daniel quickly and quietly so they could enjoy an Haute Creole lunch in the Victorian house. It was one of the famous Brennan family restaurants and that was a mark of guaranteed gustatory happiness.

CHAPTER SIXTY-TWO

Daniel took a taxi to the restaurant. He had a brief hop in his step as he bounced up the sideway to the restaurant, the blue and white striped canopy above him cheering him even further.

Telling the maître d' that he was meeting a Lauren Williams for lunch, he was immediately led to a large booth in the room to the right.

"Hello Lauren," he said expecting her to look much worse that she did. Surprisingly, she looked refreshed, well slept and even glowing.

"Hi, Daniel, would you like a drink?" nodding to the waiter that had come up from behind him.

"No, I have business meetings all day today so I only have lunch to talk to you about my search for Kathleen and hiring a private detective." He sat in the booth.

"Come closer. I don't want to have to talk too loud over

private business," she whispered.

"Certainly," he said, sliding over the banquette so they sat closely together in the center of the booth.

"How are you doing, Lauren?" he said, covering her hand in his. "When I get back to Vancouver, I am going back to the police to see if there is any progress. Unfortunately, the ship security figures that it is not their issue – that Kathleen stayed in Alaska. The Alaska police see it as a ship security issue and the RCMP see it as out of their jurisdiction. That's why I think a private detective is a good idea. This waiting is ripping me apart. How are you doing?" giving her an opening to discuss the shooting.

His false sympathy made bile rise in her throat and she took a sip of the white wine from her glass on the table.

"I can't talk about it. Maybe I can just get this paperwork done with you and then you can go back to your meetings."

She picked up the manila envelope beside her on the banquette and passed it to him over the table.

Daniel smiled and opened the envelope. *This was too easy.*

He began to peruse the documents and the smile left his face as their significance sank in.

"What the hell is this, Lauren?!"

"You could ask me that question?"

Daniel looked up to see his dead wife standing beside the table. She slid in beside Lauren. He went to move but bumped up against Sam who had slid in unnoticed beside him.

"Let me make this easy for you, Daniel," Kathleen said in a cool, calm and slow voice. "We've given the millions away to a foundation. You could try and get the board to let you manage the funds, but once I tell them about the murder attempt last night, they may be a bit reticent. The second document is my change of beneficiary for the life insurance. You will see that you have been replaced by Lauren and Sam here.

"By the way," she said in her best accountant voice, "excellent strategy on the request of life insurance equity loan. When I called to change the beneficiary, they verified the loan application details, and I was able to assure them that the loan was no longer required.

"When I return to Vancouver, I might actually get a restraining order against you. But you know how humiliating that is. They drag you into jail and then process you like a common criminal.

"To avoid that," she continued, "you will want to sign the divorce papers the second they come into your possession."

She watched his stunned face as she laid each layer of his deceit before him.

He was glad that he had decided not to return the gun.

Daniel smiled. He took his menu and propped it up on the table, sheltering the four in the booth from the gaze of other guests. Then he took the gun from its shoulder holster and put it on the table, keeping his finger loosely in the trigger hole.

"You may want to rethink this, Kathleen. I am going to put this gun in your sister's ribs and then I am going to pull the trigger. Then I am going to shoot this bitch of a reporter...."

"Writer," Sam reminded him.

"Beside me," he said ignoring Sam's squeak.

"Then I am going to shoot you between the eyes and walk out of this room."

"I don't believe so!"

What happened next occurred so quickly that Sam was hard pressed to describe it later.

Rupert had appeared beside the table, had reached over Sam

and driven his fist into Daniel's face with his right hand while grabbing the gun with his left. Tossing the gun aside, he hit Daniel again with his right and then with his left. He might have continued but Daniel was unconscious. His body was still, his face on the table, his salad fork beginning to make a pronged indentation in his cheek.

The room buzzed with shallow gasps and a few polite screams. An elderly lady pointed out the gun on the floor to her dining companion. Perhaps guns in New Orleans restaurants were rarer than one was lead to believe.

Beside Daniel, Lauren was tossed between being embarrassed by the confrontation and proud of her husband for pulverizing Daniel.

"You okay?" he asked Lauren.

"Mm hmmm," she smiled. "But can you sit down? You are making a scene."

EPILOGUE

Daniel walked off the plane and through the Vancouver airport.

After a week in a New Orleans jail, he had managed to round up the ten percent deposit for his one million dollar bail, mostly from his parents and brothers. He had been released to travel back to Canada, based on his promise to return to New Orleans for trial. If he didn't return in time, the $100,000 bail bond deposit would be forfeit.

After his luncheon date with Lauren, he had come to on the street outside Commander's Palace where Rupert and the waiter had tossed him after Rupert had punched him unconscious. One eye was swollen shut, but the other could clearly see the two officers leaning against their squad car, waiting for him to gain consciousness.

Daniel shook off the memory and then groaned where he was still sore from his contact with the street and a week on a metal bed.

He was just grateful to be back in Canada. He had spent the flight back to Vancouver fretting about how he would fix the crap hole his life had sunk into. That damn Kathleen!

He walked through the automatic doors to the baggage handling area.

"Daniel!"

Daniel looked up in response to the call of his name. Ahead of him were the two fellow investors that he had last seen at Joe Fortes. Was it only a week or so ago?

One had a printed copy of the Global Perspectives On-Line magazine in his hand. Sam's friend had done a quick job in getting the story about the foundation and the transfer of the millions into print.

"Let us buy you a drink. We insist."

Neither were smiling.

ABOUT THE AUTHOR

J. A. Martine is a pseudonym for the Canadian best-selling author Jeanne Martinson. The author lives in Saskatchewan, Canada with her husband, Malcolm.

To connect with Jeanne online, see www.j-a-martine.com

BOOKS

Fiction by Jeanne Martinson writing as J. A. Martine

If it wasn't For the Money (Sam Anderson Mystery #1)

Non-Fiction by Jeanne Martinson

Lies and Fairy Tales that Deny Women Happiness

War and Peace in the Workplace

Leadership for the 21st Century

Generation Y and the New Work Ethic

AUTHOR'S NOTE - REAL OR NOT

Have you ever visited a location you read about in a book and it was not as the author described? As I reader, I find that disconcerting. Here is the scoop on what is real and what is not:

In this book, Sam Anderson is travelling on the ship, the Sea Wanderer. There is no such ship but it is a composite of the many ships that cruise Alaska.

In Vancouver, Joe Fortes Seafood and Chop House, Chewies, and Irahai are some of Sam's and the author's favourite eating spots.

In Juneau, try the oysters at Twisted Fish and say hello to the bartender. Visit the Hearthside Bookstore for a browse. If you are up to a wee uphill walk, visit St. Nicholas Church and see how the renos are going.

In New Orleans, the Sazerac in the Roosevelt and the Carousel Bar in the Monteleone are both real and very worth the visit, as are the hotels they reside in. The history alone is worth the going, the hospitality worth the staying.

UPCOMING SAM ANDERSON TITLES

Stay Out of The Water
(Available January 2015)

The second Sam Anderson mystery finds the writer travelling western Canada to find fabulous mineral springs and spas. A dream assignment soon becomes complicated when Sam discovers a dead woman half dressed in a spa changing room. The dead woman is just a single mother with no obvious secrets or enemies, yet Sam can't help but think that someone wanted her out of the way.

Made in the USA
Charleston, SC
26 October 2014